Fa-- & Dirty

WALL STREET JOURNAL & USA TODAY BESTSELLING AUTHOR

WILLOW WINTERS

Fast & Dirty

Chapter 1

MARIE

AS MY PACE PICKS UP, SO DO THE STEPS behind me.

Following me.

Tracking me.

There's nothing to listen to on this empty street other than our echoing strides and my anxious breathing. The clacking of his shoes against the pavement resonates loud in my ears. The sound of my heels is nothing compared to the loud thuds from whoever the fuck is back there. It has to be a man. Those steps are too damn heavy to belong to anyone under two hundred pounds.

Shit. Shit. Shit.

I'm too nervous to look behind me. In the movies, when they look back, that's when they have to start running. You run or you die. Even though in most cases it's too late by that point. Anyway, I'm in no condition to run.

I'm tipsy and in three-inch black studded Jimmy Choos that my mom got me for my twenty-fifth birthday. I'm not fucking stupid; if I started running, I wouldn't make it one minute before he caught me. At least right now whoever it is back there is keeping some distance. *For now ...* I shake the unwanted thought away.

Maybe he's not following me, I tell myself over and over. He's just walking to his car or another bar; maybe he's just walking home. But after a few blocks the sound of him following me is unbearable. My heart rate picks up as the reality sets in. This isn't good. There's no way this is a coincidence.

A bad man is behind me, I know that much. There's no way in hell he's not following me. If he had good intentions, he would've said something by now. At some point he'll get closer and then I'll have to run. But I'm definitely going to make him work for it. If he wants to put his hands on me, then he's going to have to catch me and fight me. I'm not going to be a good little victim.

I wonder if I should throw down my clutch when

I take off. It might distract him for a few minutes. Maybe he's only after money. I stare down at the simple black Coach clutch hanging from my wrist. Inside is a mere twenty in cash, my dead iPhone, raspberry lip gloss, and my ID. If he makes a move, I'm dropping it ASAP. I just hope the prick sees it and decides that's what he wants.

My confidence vanishes as I hear the steps growing closer behind me. The noise brings me back to this shit reality. Who knows what the guy behind me wants, but I'll save my strength for now and continue to pray that I'm not going to be mugged … or worse. I'm not a fool; at some point I'm going to have to book it. I'm saving my energy for when that time comes.

I try to steady myself, but it's so fucking cold out, just breathing hurts. I took a cab to get here and that was a mistake. Cabs don't come around this part of town unless they're dropping you off. And my phone died before I left the bar, so I couldn't call for a ride anyway. So I'm royally fucked unless I can make it to the train station. I fucking hate taking the train, but right now I would beg on my hands and knees to be there this very second. I doubt the man behind me will let me get close to the train station. Tears prick my eyes, but I shake them off. I'm not going to cry.

I hug my shaking shoulders as best I can while keeping up my pace and try to think. My hands are freezing. My black cashmere cardigan isn't anywhere near thick enough for the cold night air and the gloves that I thought were in the pockets are now missing. I debate on whether I should rub my hands back and forth against my upper arms or shove them in my pockets. *Snap!* The sound of something being crushed underfoot behind me makes me stumble as my legs lock up in fear. I shove my hands in my pockets and will my body to keep moving forward. I keep my eyes down and watch my warm breath turn to fog while the crumbling concrete moves beneath my heels.

What the hell was I thinking, listening to Lexi? She's a flake and lately she's been a shit friend. She wanted me to meet her so she'd have a wingwoman to help her score the sexy tattoo artist who touched up her ink last week. I remember her eyes lighting up when he mentioned the dive bar he goes to nearly every night after his shift. She's such a sucker for tattooed men. And that place was filled with them. She would've been in heaven … had she bothered to show up. Well maybe not heaven, since the guy she had her heart set on was busy with some bimbo who had her breasts on full display. From the way he was staring at them you'd have thought he was having a full-on conversation with her tits.

My phone died half an hour after I got there so I have no idea why she didn't show. She could've at least answered my texts though. I waited another half hour before I took off, annoyed with my dead phone and pissed off at her. I was too angry storming out to realize I wouldn't be able to catch a cab. If this prick wasn't behind me I would've turned around and gone back to the bar to use the phone. But now I'm blocks away and this uneasy feeling won't leave me. I've made one stupid decision after another and I don't know how I'm going to get out of this fuckup I've gotten myself into.

Stupid me wanted to be a good friend. Stupid me wore the skimpy outfit she picked out for me even though it's freezing. Stupid me believed her when she said she was on her way. Stupid me didn't charge my phone. And now I'm alone in the cold, on the wrong side of town, being followed. If I make it out of this— scratch that, *when* I make it out of this—I'm going to fucking kill Lexi.

BLAKE

She's going to break her damn neck in those shoes. She carries herself well enough and it's obvious she's used to walking in heels, but the sidewalk is all cracked to shit and it's only a matter of time before she trips and lands on her pretty ass. What the hell is a girl like that even doing walking down these streets? I know she's not from around here. I knew it the second I saw her tonight, taking her sweet ass time sipping that pink drink in the shithole dive bar that's practically my second home.

I've never seen her before but I sure as shit would've noticed if I had. Those eyes, deep chocolate brown, took my fucking breath away when I caught her staring. Of course she avoided looking my way the rest of the night. That pissed me off, but whatever. She's got beautiful curves with enough of an ass on her to grab onto while I take her from behind. Her gorgeous auburn hair goes down to her waist; I could wrap it again and again around my wrist and pull her head back to bite her neck, leaving marks all over that flawless porcelain skin. Damn she's beautiful. I bet the cold is making her pale skin redden. I could do a better job of making her skin flush though. And she'd fucking love it.

She's picking up her pace, so I slow mine a bit. Not enough to let her get away, but enough to calm her ass down. I'm sure she hears me following her. I'm probably scaring the shit out of her, although I don't mean to. I also don't give a fuck—maybe it'll teach her a lesson about walking home alone in this part of town. If she'd just waited a minute longer, I would've been able to ask her if she wanted me to walk her home or call her a cab. *Or come home with me.* But fucking Jace wouldn't shut his damn mouth about the shop. Like he can't tell me about the new equipment tomorrow morning when I come in for my shift.

A beautiful piece of ass like her shouldn't be walking around here all on her own. She probably came out to go slumming, thinking she wanted something rough. A bad boy to show her a good time. I'm guessing she changed her mind when she saw her options. It's one thing to have a fantasy, but it's another thing entirely to actually get down and dirty. A tic in my jaw starts to twitch, and I clench my fists thinking that must have been exactly what she was up to.

The thought of her and some fuckface having a one-night stand pisses me off, as if I have any kind of claim on her. After a moment, I check my anger—I don't know her. I shouldn't have any opinion about who she opens her legs for … those long legs that are on full display in front of me. At least while I'm on her ass, no one's going to mess with her.

I look ahead at her and notice she's got her arms wrapped around herself. Damn, she's got to be freezing her tits off. Why'd she wear such a short dress when it's February in New York? It's cold as hell. It snowed just last week, for fuck's sake. I shake my head while I watch her turn the corner.

She's getting close to the club and that's no good. I can't be seen stalking a chick, even if I do have good intentions. The MC would never believe that shit. I've wasted too much time already, I'd better catch up to her. I can at least offer her my coat. She's got to be frozen enough to accept that, even if she is scared shitless.

Chapter 2

MARIE

ADRENALINE STARTS RACING THROUGH ME and I practically suffocate from my heart jumping up my throat. I turn the corner and gun it, sprinting as fast as I can in these damn heels. If they didn't have buckles, I'd have taken them off or left them behind. But being fucking brilliant, I wore shoes with buckles around the ankles.

"Shit!" I hear the man behind me swear and the thudding of his boots gets louder and closer together. *Fuck!* I push with everything I have, running on the balls of my feet so I don't trip like a dumbass and make it easy for the asshole behind me. He's closing in on me. Tears prick my eyes again, but I force them back. *I knew this would happen. Shit.* My heart is beating out of my chest and the heated sweat coating my neck is at odds with the freezing cold air battering my exposed skin. I take ragged breaths and they send sharp pains down my lungs. It's too cold for this shit. I pump my arms, trying to go faster as he comes up behind me. I scream and flail as his arms wrap around my waist and he pulls me into his muscular body.

"Hold up. Just-" His deep baritone voice is sexy as hell, but I don't listen. Fuck that. I throw my elbow into his side and it makes contact exactly where I need it to. His arms release their hold just enough for me to wiggle free and land on the balls of my feet. I don't hesitate, not for one second. Even with my hair in my face, I take off stumbling.

My heels slam ruthlessly against the cold concrete as I turn back to catch a glimpse, hoping the prick is still stunned. Fuck, he's huge. If he wasn't pissed before, he's going to be pissed now. My anxiety spikes again and the rush of blood in my ears is so fast and loud I can't hear a damn thing. My muscles are already burning, but I push through the pain and run like my life depends on it. I look back again and I'm struck by the sensation of running right into a brick wall. A brick wall of solid muscle. Muscle that's holding me so tight it's going to squeeze the life out of me.

I try to scream, but a hand moves over my mouth, practically covering my entire face. My body starts to shake as I scream helplessly and attempt to break free. Nothing. It's no use. *No, no, not like this.* Through the tears threatening to fall, I see a blurred vision of the man who was following me. I try to break free again but the hulk of a man holding me makes it impossible. Tears burn down my face. It's hopeless.

BLAKE

Out of all the people to run into, it had to be Maddox. She couldn't just listen to me, could she? I shouldn't have let her get so far ahead. I shouldn't have let her walk off on her own in the first place.

She got a good hit in, I'll give her that. But then she had to run straight into him. My nerves start getting the better of me, but I can't let it show. Snatching up girls isn't his style. He'd break his own neck before he laid an unwanted hand on a woman. Not only is it not necessary since he gets the pick of the litter at the clubhouse, being VP and all, but it's also too risky. Too easy to get caught doing stupid shit when you have bigger things to hide. I can't have him thinking that I'm into that kind of shit. But fuck, this looks bad.

"Blake," he gives me an asymmetrical grin as he nods in greeting, "I think I just caught your kitten."

I snort a laugh in response as I finally reach them. He's a big motherfucker and his size makes her look all the smaller. I've still got a few inches and pounds on him, but it's not just his size that makes Maddox a threat. It's his connections, his power. That, and how ruthless he is. He may be smiling now, but he smiles just the same as he puts a bullet in a man's skull. I know, I've been right by his side, giving the same fucking smile to the poor bastard.

Her feet are barely even touching the ground with the way he's got her held up. He doesn't have to man-handle her like that. Well maybe he does since she's a spitfire, but I still don't fucking like it.

"I wouldn't call her a kitten," I say and give him a forced lopsided grin as I add, "she's more of a hellcat." He laughs like I told him the funniest joke he's ever heard. I can't help but notice that she's quietened down and gone still and seems to be listening. Good, I've got her attention. I have to think quick to get both of us out of this mess. I can't trust him with this, even if he's basically my brother. Seeing as how he's right outside the club, he could have anyone with him, friend or foe, and an innocent like her shouldn't be around either.

"My hellcat wanted to spice things up and try something different tonight. We were just heading home to try out a little roleplay. You know I don't usually mind, but I'm not planning on sharing her."

His eyes narrow like he doesn't believe a word out of my mouth. Yeah I'm lying, but he can't know that for sure. He wouldn't know if I'm seeing someone. We don't talk about that shit. Besides, women come and go with us. And I never hold one down. Never. I can't bring them into this.

"Come on baby, stop fighting him. Maddox's not getting your ass tonight and I bet all that wiggling in his arms got him hard." It's fucking difficult keeping calm and I make sure to keep my grin on my face. My nerves are shot to hell. I can't fuck this up. Years of work would be wasted. It's work I don't give two shits about and I'm pretty sure the execs of the MC are onto me anyway, but if they aren't then this could really cause problems. Life or death problems. Hopefully she figures out what the hell is going on and that I'm not a threat.

If she doesn't we're both fucked.

Chapter 3

MARIE

WHAT THE FUCK IS GOING ON? I TRY TO clear my head and push down the overwhelming need to vomit as I get a good grip on the situation. Breathing's hard, but I concentrate on taking advantage of the little bit of air I can get through the thick fingers pressed against my mouth. The man in front of me, Blake, is fucking huge. His broad chest and muscular arms are on display with his Henley stretched taut. I could get lost in those steely blue eyes. He's got a bit of a beard, brunette hair that's just long enough to grab on to and tattoos scrolling up his neck on one side, making him look like a cold-blooded badass who'd fuck your shit up without hesitation.

Or pin your legs back and fuck you like he owns you.

I recognize him as the tears in my eyes finally clear. He was at the bar with Lexi's crush. That knowledge drops my fear levels down a notch. At least I've seen him before. I don't know who the fuck this guy holding me is. And I'm sure as hell not okay with it. As soon as I get a chance I'm elbowing him right in his dick. I happen to know right where it is, since it's digging into my back.

I realize I've stopped fighting while I was staring at Blake. He's got a stupid grin on his face like the cat who caught the canary.

" … more of a hellcat." Damn right I am. I'm racking my brain trying to figure out what the hell I'm going to do. I attempt to move again, but the brute of a man holding me has yet to loosen his grip.

"My hellcat wanted to spice things up and try something different tonight. We were just heading home to try out a little roleplay. You know I don't usually mind, but I'm not planning on sharing her."

His voice is calm and confident. My heart fucking stops at the thought of being shared by these two. Not going to fucking happen. Even though my pussy just clenched in longing and my core is instantly hot.

Is that what the guy holding me wants? No fucking way. I start to fight again when I hear Blake speak up through a laugh.

"Come on baby, stop fighting him. Maddox's not getting your ass tonight and I bet all that wiggling in his arms got him hard." I look at him once more and something in his eyes is pleading with me to play along. For some strange reason, I feel an instant sense of safety with him. It's fucking crazy. I was just running for my life to get away from him, but now my body is pushing me to trust him.

Danger. I can feel it in every bone of my body. Whoever this Maddox is must be a threat. It makes sense if Blake has me playing a role. Maddox is a danger to Blake too. Although I don't see how anyone could be a danger to Blake; he looks like a man who gets what he wants and would slice your throat open if you stood in his way.

I don't have many options as it is. But if he's giving me a way to go from having to fight two men off to only having to fight him ... I'll take it. I force myself to relax in Maddox's arms, which is difficult since his body against mine keeps me on high alert. He's holding me like he's done this before and I can't get away from the deep rumbling of his chest when he speaks. It's scary as hell.

I may have grown up a naïve little girl, but I know better now. I need to play along and take the out that Blake's given me. At least for the moment. I mumble into Maddox's hand to let me down. Not that he can hear what the hell I'm saying. But it gets a laugh from both of the men and the brick shithouse finally lets me loose.

My first instinct is to run when he sets me down, but my legs are shaking too much. I shut down that train of thought and instead attempt to right myself and get into the mindset Blake wants me to be in. I'm his hellcat. That thought sends an instant wave of desire through me. My treacherous body can't get past the fact that he's ripped and sexy as fuck.

I look up at Blake and whimper, "I think I hurt my ankle." I try to sound a bit sexy and pout a little. I want this fucker to think I may actually be hurt *and* that I'm playing along with him. My heart's still pounding in my throat and I'm just hoping I read him right.

"Aw shit, let me take a look." He sounds sincere in his response and walks over with purpose, staring at the ankle I'm holding.

I think back to when he caught me on the street.

Why the hell was he chasing me if he wasn't going to hold me down and have his way with me or mug me or whatever the fuck he had in mind? Why not let this Maddox guy have me? Why not let him join in? My filthy mind almost takes over and I have to push it down and rid my head of those thoughts before I lose my shit.

BLAKE

I drop to the ground and take her calf in my hands and slowly slide my fingers down to her ankle. There's a strap buckled around it, but it doesn't look swollen. I put a little pressure just under the bone. She doesn't even flinch at my touch. I look up at her to gauge her pain, but I swear my heart stops beating.

She's fucking gorgeous. She's panting a little and her lips are swollen from being held so tight, but I can tell that's how they would look if I were to give her a brutal kiss while fucking her. She'd be panting and writhing beneath me while I gave her just the right mix of pain and pleasure. My dick hardens instantly and I force back a groan.

I have to clear my throat to ask, "Does that hurt?" Those chocolate eyes find mine and she nods her head gently, her locks swaying across her shoulders. She's playing me. Her ankle doesn't fucking hurt. That's alright though, I'm playing her too. Tit for tat I guess.

I harden my voice a bit and search out Maddox, who's still behind my little hellcat. "Maddox, can you get me a chair real quick?" He stares back at me and his brow furrows.

"Why don't you just bring her in?" Fuck, I didn't think of that. Why wouldn't I bring her in? The clubhouse is less than ten feet away and it's a lot fucking warmer in there. I've got to be smarter than this.

"I don't really wanna stick around and I swear if I see Jace in there I'm going to knock him the fuck out." Maddox laughs at that. "He never shuts the fuck up."

"I hear ya." He turns toward the back doors which are propped open with a brick. "You want a drink, little kitten?" That nickname pisses me the fuck off. She's not his kitten.

She turns her attention toward him and in a syrupy sweet voice answers, "No thanks, Maddox," as if she's known him her whole life. Like they didn't just meet five minutes ago.

He looks at me and raises his brows questioningly. I answer easily, "I'm good." He nods and goes on his way inside. Not five seconds after he's gone, she starts acting up again. I feel her stiffen as my hand grips her calf. I'm not fucking stupid. She wants to fight me and take off again. I can see it happening before she gets a chance to move.

I look up at her and growl, "Don't fucking kick me and run." Her eyes widen and her whole body goes still. *Yeah, I'm onto you, hellcat.* "You wouldn't get far and it would be a very, very bad move on your part. Understand?" She clenches her teeth, but nods and I can't help but to add, "Good girl." I run my fingers down the inside of her knee, petting her.

"What's your name?" I stare into her gorgeous brown eyes, willing her to give me the truth.

"Marie."

"Marie," I repeat and let the soft word linger on my tongue, tasting it. I nod my head, liking the sound. "Just a few more minutes Marie, then I'll take you home." She stares back at me with disbelieving eyes that are slowly narrowing with anger and defiance. I chuckle, deep and low. "Your home, hellcat. I was just going to walk you home."

Chapter 4

BLAKE

CAN TELL SHE ISN'T BUYING IT AND THAT CUTE little mouth parts to no doubt tell me she doesn't believe that shit—even though it's true. But she stops when she hears the door to the club open. And that disbelief is exactly why I had to lie to the VP and put on this charade. All because I had some stupid urge to look out for her.

I look back to Maddox and he's got Pinch and Linc with him too. Marie turns and sees them and her whole body goes rigid. I move to stand in front of her and rub my hand along her body as I do. Just for the fun of it mostly, feeling her smooth skin beneath my fingertips. When I get to her ass I pause and move slowly to just below her waist. Her eyes widen at my touch and I chuckle again while rubbing small circles on her lower back.

I whisper for her to relax before giving her a small open-mouth kiss in the crook of her neck. It's all for show of course, but I'll be damned if I didn't enjoy every second of it. I can't help my growl when she lets out a small moan and clenches her thighs. That's not helping to get rid of this hard-on. But it's doing wonders for the act I'm putting on. As long as this charade looks real to them for the next five minutes before we can take off, we'll be fine. They'll think she's just some kinky hookup and all will be right again. I readjust myself before parting with her to meet the guys. It's a risk, knowing she could take off. But something in me is urging me to give her this. To show her I trust her to trust me. So I leave her a few steps behind as I approach Linc and give him a cocky grin.

"What the hell are you doing here?" As I ask him casually, I hear her walk up to me and she slowly molds her body to mine. I wrap an arm around her shoulder and let her place her head on my chest while she sizes up the other guys. She's doing a good job of playing her part. I'm not sure what her plan is, but I'm loving her little touches. I don't know if she's even aware that she's gently scratching her nails down my back, but the act she's putting on is making my dick throb even harder for her.

Maybe she's starting to believe that I was going to walk her home. I hope she does believe me 'cause that would make all this shit that much easier. I breathe in deep and take in her sweet honeysuckle scent. I have to remind myself that she's just trying to survive—like me. Without that reminder, my dick would take over. A soft growl rumbles out of me at the thought.

"Maddox said you had a girl out here. I had to see it to believe it."

I smile back at him. "What, like I couldn't get a girl?"

"There's a difference between pussy and a girl." Marie hardens against me, her brow furrowed and lips pursed. She obviously doesn't like the fact that they may see her as just a piece of ass. To be honest, I don't like that idea either, even though for her sake it would be best for them to believe it. She shifts against me and I can tell she's debating on leaving. I've got to nip that in the bud.

"Marie, this is Linc, my boss."

She smirks and relaxes back into me before nodding. "I remember you telling me about him. Nice to meet you, Linc." Damn, that lie came off flawless. I almost forget to keep a smile on my face. I'll add that to the things I know about Marie. Hellcat knows how to fight, she's a good liar, and she's sexy as fuck. So far I like the list.

"Marie, nice to meet you too. I was wondering when Blake was going to introduce us." Fucking Linc—trying to make me look good. He's like the father I never had. Always looking out for me. He hired me in the tattoo shop and taught me everything I needed to know. Now he's trying to get me brownie points like I've been talking about her for awhile now or something. That'd be nice of him if I hadn't learned her name two minutes ago. It's hard to keep my laugh in. Hellcat doesn't even try to hold it back.

"Oh yeah, Blake's been talking about me?" She raises her brows and gives another sweet smirk toward Linc. She looks back at me and pats my chest condescendingly. "I don't believe it." She leans closer to them before whispering loud enough for me to hear, "He's not big on commitment." This time I lose my composure and let the hurt show on my face. The four of them are laughing at her little joke until she notices my butthurt expression.

"Aw, babe. I didn't mean it. I'm just surprised you're

telling your friends about me since it's only been a couple of weeks." She's really fucking good at this. My curiosity is piqued. Before I can play along more, Maddox interrupts.

"You need anything for that ankle, kitten?"

I'm gonna have to let the kitten remark go, but I still don't fucking like it coming from Maddox's mouth. We've shared before, but I'm not sharing her. I position her in front of me. And then I pull her back against my chest while wrapping my arms around her tiny waist. It's a possessive hold and the guys take notice. She may not be my old lady, but she's not a groupie up for grabs.

"Nope," she replies all peppy, like she isn't in any danger at all. I'm hoping that's because I'm wrapped around her like a vine. I push her back against my cock and let her feel how fucking hard she's made me. I hear her little gasp before she adds in a breathy voice, "It must've been the damn buckle on my heel." I grin, letting my head rest on hers. I know this didn't start out well, but I'll die a little inside if I don't get into her pussy tonight. I need a taste of my hellcat.

Pinch looks at her like a predator and licks his lower lip as he asks, "So you two were having a little chase?" She goes rigid in my arms. I can't blame her. I'm not worried though. Pinch has some serious kinks, but he's never crossed the line with a woman. Not that I've seen anyway, and there's nothing on his record. None of them have done any shit like that. Given the way they treat women, it's been easier than I thought it would be to keep this job.

The MC's illegal activities keep my head in the game. That's why I agreed to go undercover. Being back on American soil wasn't treating me well after the shit I went through overseas. I needed to focus on something worth fighting for and the idea of busting their group for peddling drugs and guns did just that for me. But so far all I've seen is underground fighting. It's fucking brutal and they make a shit ton of money, but I don't see a problem with it. I fucking live for it now.

I smirk at Pinch and reply, "That's none of your fucking business." His crazy ass grin covers his face. "Like I told Maddox, I'm not sharing this one." Pinch laughs and nods his head.

He waggles his brows at my hellcat though. "If you change your mind, I love a little chase."

She gives him a skeptical look before he adds, "I like to be the one running away though." She laughs at him and I shake my head. At least he's putting her at ease now. She leans back against me, rubbing her ass along my cock. God, I hope this isn't all just a pretense for her.

"Next time, keep it off the streets, Blake." Maddox looks at me with an admonishing stare. I nod. I'm just grateful this fucking worked and that I'll be able to wrap it up soon and get her ass where it belongs.

"Yeah, I got it." Just as we're about to make our way out, the damn hellcat in my arms decides she doesn't like me being scolded.

"Why the hell is that, Maddox?" Her voice is the epitome of defiance. My eyes widen almost as much as Maddox's. He tilts his head as if daring her to keep it up. I can't help the fact that her feistiness makes me that much harder, not helping the situation at all.

"If I want to enjoy a little rough play, I don't see why Blake can't give it to me." Hearing those words come out of her sweet little mouth nearly knocks me on my ass. *Oh baby, I can give it to you. You'll be begging to let me give you that fantasy.* Maddox holds his hands up in defeat and the rest of the guys laugh.

"You weren't kidding," he says then looks right at me with a smirk, "she is a little hellcat."

After a few minutes of shooting the shit while Linc finishes up his cigarette, I go to leave so I can get my little hellcat out of here and hopefully under me. Just for a little taste.

"We're gonna take off. I'll see you guys later." I turn her in my arms to leave, giving the guys a nod.

"Hold up, you guys aren't heading in?" It's only around eleven so it makes sense that we'd be going to the club, but I have to shoot Linc down.

"Nah, I have a little chasing to do." I shoot Marie a wicked grin and groan when she responds by biting her lip while a blush creeps up her chest and into her cheeks.

"Aw, but we just met you, kitten," Pinch says and smiles at her. "Don't you wanna come see the club?" Then he actually pouts at her. *What the fuck?* I don't like this possessive shit that's come over me. I'm fully aware that he's just fucking around, but I want to punch his face in for flirting with her. As I'm contemplating doing just that, my hellcat throws a wrench in my plan to get her out of here.

"Yeah, sure," she begins and looks me right in the eyes as she says sweet as can be, "We can go in for a little while, can't we, Blake?" *Fuck me.*

Chapter 5

MARIE

MAYBE I CAN BLAME IT ALL ON SHOCK. That's why my head isn't working right.

Call me a fool, but I feel more safe wrapped in Blake's arms than I've felt in years. Even worse, I don't want to let that feeling go. I hope this isn't all an act on his part. It can't be. He has to be feeling this connection too. It'll destroy me if he denies it.

It's not the alcohol making me want him, I know that. I haven't felt the desire to be touched by a man in over a year, and God knows I've gotten drunk at bars and had plenty of good-looking men try. But with Blake, my body is begging me to let him have his way with me. I want him to take me. Claim me. Own my body. I can tell he knows how to do just that and at this point, I'd happily get on my knees for him.

In fact, if his lips touch that sweet spot on my neck just one more time, my legs will probably give out as my body shudders and spasms from cumming so damn hard. I'm that close to my release. I keep scissoring my legs together, but it's not enough. I need his touch. Even if it's just a little. Feeling his hard cock against my ass, the rumble of his chest as he tried to hide his groan when I pushed back against him—how could I not be hot for him? I enjoy being his hellcat and right now I just want to purr for him.

BLAKE

I grab her shoulder right before we get to the entrance to the clubhouse, letting the guys go in without us. She stumbles a little before falling back into my chest, but she smiles up at me as I wrap my arms around her waist. I guide her to the side of the building. She doesn't try to push away; instead she leans into me, grabbing hold of my arm to keep her balance on the broken concrete.

"What's your angle, hellcat?" I keep my face emotionless and get right to the point.

"What do you mean?" She looks innocent and genuinely confused.

"You think I'm gonna hurt you? Is that why you wanna go in there?" She stumbles back from me like I slapped her. Her eyes widen and I want to kick my own ass for putting that wounded expression on her face.

"No, I just-" she looks to the ground as she tries to find her words. I grab her chin with my thumb on her bottom lip and force her to look at me. Those chocolate brown eyes look deep into mine with pure lust as I move my nose to hers, my lips just barely touching hers.

"You just what?" I stare straight into her eyes, willing her to give me the green light.

"I just want you," she whispers and the second she does I move in, pushing her body against the brick building, caging her in. She moans as my lips take hers in a bruising kiss. I bite her bottom lip before my tongue pushes into her hot, wet mouth. My hands travel along her body, reaching below her dress and cupping her pussy. She moans into my mouth as my fingers rub against her. She wants this just as much as I do. I can't help the groan that escapes me.

I rip her skimpy lace panties off and while my

fingertips dig into the flesh of her hips, I growl into her neck, "Beg me."

I feel her pussy gush against my thigh; I know she left her honey on my jeans and that gets my dick impossibly harder. She doesn't hesitate to beg, "Please fuck me, Blake. I need you."

Thank fuck. I lift her up as I struggle to release my cock from my jeans. Her legs wrap around me as I position the head of my cock at her hot entrance and mercilessly slam into her balls deep.

"Fuck!" she screams out and throws her head back against the brick wall. She's so damn hot and tight. The sight of her being consumed by pleasure with her eyes half-lidded and plump lips parted in ecstasy is the sexiest thing I've ever fucking seen. I pause for just a second to let her adjust to my size and feel her clench around my dick. *Fuck yeah.* Her pussy feels like heaven as she tries to milk my cock with her orgasm.

I pound into her little pussy and she tries to quiet her screams by biting her lip, but she's failing miserably. As much as I want to hear her cry out while I destroy her pussy, I don't want any of those fuckers coming out here to watch. *She's mine.* "Bite my shoulder." She immediately clamps down on me and that bit of pain combined with her pulsing pussy is almost enough to make me cum already. I have to fight hard not to give in just yet. I haven't had enough and I've got to give her more.

Her heels dig into my ass, begging me to take her harder. So I do just that. I'm rutting into her with a primal need. We're both panting as I keep a steady pace and move my hand to her clit, pressing down ruthlessly as I feel her body start to shake. I know she's going to be quick again and I love how damn responsive she is. She's so fucking wet I can feel her arousal dripping down to my balls. The sounds of me pounding into her wet pussy make me fuck her harder, racing to my climax.

She releases my shoulder just enough to beg me breathlessly, "Please, Blake." Her panted plea takes me over the edge and I bite down hard on her neck while slamming into her to the hilt and pinching her clit.

She screams into my neck before biting down on my shoulder with such force that I know she draws blood. The pain makes me cum even more, filling her tight pussy until it's leaking out of her.

As I come down from my orgasm, I hear the door to the clubhouse open.

Fuck.

How the hell can I bring her into the clubhouse, into my world knowing the danger I'll be putting her in? I move my forehead from hers, hearing her little pants as her aftershocks settle and her eyes pierce into mine; it's too late. She's mine now. I'm not letting her go.

Chapter 6

MADDOX

"I DON'T KNOW, PRES." I ANSWER LINC honestly while I look through the office window across the clubhouse at Marie. She's at the bar with Blake and he's practically pissing circles around her. He's marking his territory like he's going to make her his old lady.

There are a few women lingering, but they look nothing like Marie. Most of them are desperate for attention and clinging onto anyone they can. It's never bothered me before, but seeing Marie all calm in Blake's embrace with an air of confidence and ease surrounding her … Well, I want that. Remembering the sounds of her begging, I adjust my hardening dick and hold back my groan.

In the clubhouse we're used to hearing and seeing all manner of fucking. But damn, hearing Blake pound into her … If I weren't worried about Blake and what the hell he's doing, I'd have made my presence known and helped her get off. And then again. I press my lips into a thin line, wondering how Blake would've acted. I glance back up at them and his arm is around her shoulder while he whispers in her ear. My eyes fall to the floor.

"He'd be stupid to bring someone from his past around. He knows the risk." I clench my teeth at Linc's words.

I speak up, "I didn't take him for a piece of shit who'd risk a girl like that." Looking back at Linc, I can tell that thought pisses him off too. It'd be fucked up to put your girl in danger. Especially when you're an undercover cop infiltrating an MC.

Why the hell would he think it's safe to get a girl? If his cover was blown—even though we already know— he would have to know that we'd use her against him. Not that we would, but some other clubs might. He shouldn't have taken the risk. I look back at Pres while he's nodding his head at my words. "I swear to God it looked like he was up to no good the way she was fighting him. No way I would've guessed they were just fucking around." I have to admit that a possessive hold ran through me when I saw that shit. I grabbed onto her like a damn lifeline while I stared my partner down. I would've knocked his ass out if I'd let go of her. I shake my head, not knowing what the fuck that feeling running through me is all about.

"None of this matches what we know about him." Linc's words come out hard and I can tell that he isn't happy that we didn't know this shit about Blake. He's like my brother. If he wasn't a cop, I'd put my life on the line for him. Shit, I'd be lying if I said I wouldn't risk my life for him now. Even knowing he's lied straight to my face. The thought makes me clench my fists tighter, turning my knuckles white. I can't help that it fucking hurts.

When he first came to us, it was like tryouts. Not that he knew. His superior sent him to us so we could see if we wanted him. If not, he'd call him off. We've had Roger in our back pocket for a while now. He told us Blake was a former marine and sniper.

Hell yeah we could use someone with his skills. Having him onboard has made deliveries run a lot smoother. Motherfuckers don't mess with you when they know they'd fall to the ground dead before their men even got their weapons out. One asshole thought he'd pull a gun on us once, fucker got a bullet in his hand before he could pull it completely out of his holster. Word gets around. Having Blake has made everything a piece of cake for the past two years. Linc's been talking about making Blake sergeant at arms for over a year now. He fucking deserves it. Except that he's a goddamn cop.

His first week, I fucked up. We're supposed to keep a low profile when we have a new prospect around, especially one that could rat us out. An asshole who wanted into the club, not even a fucking candidate yet, started smacking around one of the women. That's not something you do in our clubhouse.

She told him no and for some reason he seemed to forget what no meant. My dad didn't know what no meant either, and I got a little carried away remembering all that shit. Especially when I saw the prick backhand her so hard across the face, her lip split and she fell to the ground. I was drunk and angry. No one tried to hold me back though. They knew that asshole had it coming. I didn't stop smashing him into the wall until I heard his head crack. Didn't kill him though, just sent him into a coma. I used to have some anger issues. I'm a bit better now. A tiny bit. I was sorry for all of five minutes until Pinch told me the guy was wanted in another state for beating his last girlfriend into the ER.

Anyway, we kept waiting to hear back from Roger. Blake saw the whole thing. Helped us clean up and get rid of the prick's unconscious ass. It was only a matter of time before he said something. But weeks passed and nothing, not a fucking peep. We even told Roger to question him specifically on any violent activity. Blake never said a damn word about it. Confused the hell out of me. I liked the fucker right off the bat, but I didn't trust him.

I snicker at the thought—how the fuck could I trust a cop? I couldn't help but to question Blake about it. I asked him what he thought about what happened. He said he was glad it was me who'd grabbed the asshole because he didn't know if he'd have been able to stop. It's been a little more than a year and a half since then. Every day I like the fucker more but it pisses me off that he hasn't told us the truth. Some days I swear I just want to ask him outright and see if he'd lie straight to my face.

I stare down at the papers again. One for him and

the new one, still hot from the printer, is hers. "You got her name from her ID, Pinch?"

"Yeah, too fucking easy to grab it. I gotta figure out how to put it back though. Blake's not budging an inch now that they're inside." I snort at his response and look back down at the papers. His words run through me again. *Not sharing this one.* A scowl grows on my face.

"Nothing links them. Not a damn thing." I shake my head. She's got to be a new girl. No way she's someone from his past. But no way she's a cop either. Pinch is damn good at what he does and if he says she's legit, then she's legit.

"He said they started seeing each other a few weeks ago?" Pres asks again.

"Technically, she did."

"But Jace didn't say shit about him sneaking around with a girl, did he?"

"Not that he told us." I shake my head.

"Get his ass in here." Linc's pissed off. I don't blame him. Pres always liked Blake, but he's also always known everything about him and what he's doing. I don't know why he hasn't told Blake that we know what he is and that we want him in our back pocket just like Roger. I'm not looking forward to the day when I'm going to have to stare down my brother and tell him I knew he'd been lying to me since the beginning.

Then again, I'd be telling that to a man who's saved my life half a dozen times and even helped kill my fucked up father and bury his abusive ass. He didn't tell his super about that either. We didn't even tell Pres. I shake off the unwanted emotions creeping up on me.

Blake's a good guy, but why the hell he'd bring a girl in fully knowing the risks is beyond me. I'm having a hard time wrapping my head around that. He shouldn't have brought her around. He shouldn't have risked her. Part of me wants to go out there and kick his ass for doing that shit. But then he'd know that I know. *This is so fucked.*

"Yes, sir." I shoot a text over to Jace, who walked into the club a few minutes ago hammered. So much for keeping an eye on the cop.

I think back to when I caught her running from him. "For what it's worth, he looked pissed when I grabbed her. He covered it up quick," I say and let out a sigh, "but he wasn't happy that I had my hands on her."

"No shit." Linc looks at me like I'm a damn idiot. "Would you like it if another man had their hands on your girl?" I smirk. No fucking way.

"Yo, Pres." Jace barrels in the door and nods his greeting. "Veep, what's going on, guys?" He takes a seat across from Linc, to my left.

"Who's Marie, Jace?" Linc jumps right into it. He doesn't like to waste time.

"Who the hell is Marie?" His drunk ass looks confused. I shake my head and run my hands down my face. Yeah we like Blake, but Jace is supposed to watch him. He should know what's going on. The look on Linc's face tells me he agrees and he's fucking furious. He tilts his head to crack his neck on both sides and then stretches out his shoulders, all the while looking right at Jace. I can't help but smirk, hiding it behind my hand. Jace shrinks back into his seat and gains some sort of composure. The three of us and Pinch are the only ones who know Blake's a cop and we all let loose around him, but Jace should be following orders. It's his job to keep an eye on what Blake's doing. Especially since they spend nearly every day together at the tattoo shop.

"Has Blake had a girl around lately?" I ask, trying to ease some of the tension.

"No, nothing's changed." Jace looks right at me, avoiding the Pres' hard stare boring into his head.

"You're supposed to keep your eyes on him." Linc's firm voice grabs Jace's attention.

"He's patched, Pres; we were just having a few drinks."

I purse my lips. Yeah he's patched, but that shouldn't matter. We patched him last week, 'cause, well fuck, 'cause we like him. He's more of a brother to me than half the guys in this club. I wish Pres would just tell him we know already. It's like he has fun fucking with him. At least he was until tonight.

"I don't give a fuck if he's patched. I told you to watch him and you obviously weren't watching enough to see that he was bringing a woman around."

"If you'd told me that's what I was supposed to be watching for, then I'd have noticed. What's the deal with the chick anyway, what's she look like?"

"I don't have to tell you shit, Jace." Linc's losing his shit. I look to him and narrow my eyes. When he nods, giving me the go-ahead to take over, I lean into Jace.

"The chick's not the issue. Why the hell would he bring someone around that we could use against him if we," I wave my hands in the air and roll my eyes, "found out that he's a cop?"

Jace looks like he's contemplating an answer and

then starts shaking his head as he says, "He wouldn't do that."

I give him a blank stare and point out, "He did." I gesture to the window. "He's staking his claim on her right now."

"No shit, he's gonna have an old lady?" Jace asks in wonder while leaning over to get a look.

I look right at Linc and ask, "Does he know that we know?" Before he can answer me, Jace yells out.

"No fucking way, I know her." We stare at him, waiting for him to continue. "She's friends with that chick."

My stare turns hard. *Fucking Jace.* "A little more specific, asshole."

"Just some chick who came in to touch up her tattoo. Her friend's name is Lexi. Hot little piece. I've been looking out for her at the bar, but she hasn't shown up yet." He clucks his tongue. After a minute he shakes his head. "He hasn't been seeing her. She came to the bar tonight looking lost and left about an hour ago, all pissed off for some reason. He was with me and didn't say a word to her the whole time."

"What the hell?"

"Yeah, there's no way she's his girl." He leans over, looking out the window again and adds, "Well, she wasn't his girl a couple of hours ago." The thought that she's not *that* attached to him makes me grin. It lasts only a few seconds as I realize what I'm thinking is fucked up. I can't do that to Blake. What the fuck's gotten into me?

"You sure, Jace?" He nods his head at Pres' question. "Alright then, keep an eye on him tonight. No more fucking around."

Pinch strolls in just as Jace is leaving. "Got off the phone with Roger." He plops down in a seat by the window and looks out at the main room before looking back at us to ask, "What?"

"What do you mean, 'what?'" I can't hide my irritation. They're so fucking relaxed about this. I'm gonna end up punching one of these fuckheads in the damn jaw.

"Why are you all staring at me?" He's genuinely confused. Like we're not all waiting to hear what Blake's supervisor had to say.

"Well, what the fuck did Roger say?" I practically snarl at him, but Pinch being the psycho that he is, he just smiles at me like a fool.

"Ooh," he says and lets out his signature crazy ass laugh. I swear to God his mom dropped him on his head too many times. "I told you she's not a cop." He's all confident with a huge grin on his face. "He's never seen her or heard of her."

"Why the hell would she lie?" She said they'd been together for weeks. For some reason the thought of her lying to me hurts almost as much as Blake lying.

"The more important question is, why would he lie to us?" Pinch makes a good point. "He's never lied to us before." I tilt my head at him, giving him a pointed look. "Well, not outright to our faces."

Chapter 7

MARIE

"YOU KEEP STARING AT ME, AND IT'S STARTING to freak me out." I can't help but to call Blake out. We've been at the bar watching ESPN for the last half an hour or so, but I keep feeling his eyes on me. Well, we're not really watching TV. We've been chatting about the MC and the fight coming up tomorrow, but I've been keeping my eyes on the TV. I can't look at him without getting wet and imagining what we must've looked like while he fucked me against the wall. A blush creeps up my cheeks and Blake knows exactly what I'm thinking if his rough chuckle is any indication. I sink into the seat a little more, getting comfortable. Whatever, he knows I fucking loved it.

"I like looking

at you." His easy reply makes me smile. "I'm just wondering what the hell you were doing tonight." I give Blake a questioning look. "Were you looking for trouble?"

I scrunch up my nose and say, "No, I don't need trouble in my life." Fuck that, I finally got trouble *out* of my life.

"Then why the hell did you say you wanted to come here?"

"Well, they asked and I was following your lead." I raise my voice a bit and he chuckles again before leaning into me, putting his hand on my upper thigh and squeezing. His thumb runs soothing circles against my bare skin. He gives me a small kiss on the cheek and whispers, "Calm down, hellcat. We aren't out of the fire yet." I fucking love the feel of his lips on me. His hands.

"I don't understand. If you're a part of their club, then why did you lie?"

"It's complicated." I laugh at his short response. I bet it is. If you're lying to the people you're supposed to trust most ... well, then something is truly fucked.

"But I don't get it. Is there something between you and Maddox?"

"Naw. He's basically my brother." He shakes his head and leans back a bit to take another swig of his beer. I want to know more about the two of them, but he changes the subject.

"You were freaked out, yeah?" I nod, of course I was. "Well, the club would not be okay with what it looked like. I would not be okay and neither would you if they thought the police would be called. I had to think fast to keep both of us from getting into deep shit with Maddox."

I shake my head and say, "You could've just told me." I wish he'd come up to me earlier while I was waiting on Lexi. This whole night would've gone so much better. Well, maybe not. I purse my lips. I probably would've just pushed him away. I clench my thighs together and close my eyes at the tantalizing ache. And then none of this would've happened. That would've been a damn shame.

"I tried and you almost took out my spleen," he jokes. I can't help but smile. I didn't hold back either; I know that shit hurt.

"You didn't have to grab me." I eye him playfully and give him a sexy smirk before picking up my own beer. It's a Belgian white. It's alright. I prefer vodka to beer though. The clubhouse isn't really stacked on girl drinks, even though there are a few other girls in here.

"What the hell was I supposed to do when you

were running for your life a block away from the club? You're lucky it was me who followed you out of that bar." I bite the inside of my cheek. He's right. I still need to try to get hold of Lexi. Tonight could've gone horribly wrong if it hadn't been Blake behind me.

"Whatever, I wouldn't have called the cops anyway." His forehead creases at my flippant response. Like he doesn't believe me. Or maybe it pisses him off. It's hard to tell with the way his eyes are narrowing.

"So if Maddox hadn't caught you and you'd gotten away from me, you wouldn't have called the cops?"

"Nope," I answer easily. He looks at me like I'm fucking crazy. I put my bottle down and stare him straight in the eyes. "The police don't do shit. They wouldn't help me anyway." *I should know.*

"What's that about the police?" That big, sexy fucker Maddox and their friend Pinch sneak up behind us. Maddox's rough voice scares the shit out of me, making me jump. I think about his muscular arms holding me against his hard chest and I have to look away to hide my blush when I remember Blake saying something about how they share.

Shit. It can't be good that I'm talking about the police in an MC clubhouse. I look to Blake but he seems just fine, grinning as he takes another swig. He's obviously amused at the fact that Maddox scares me. I hope he can't tell that I'm hot for him too. The thought makes me feel a little guilty. I'm not that kind of girl. Then again, I'm also not the kind that gets fucked outside against a building. Blake turns on his barstool and positions his leg between Maddox and me.

"She was just saying that police don't do shit," he states matter-of-factly, not the least bit fazed.

"Why's that?" Maddox looks at me like he really wants to know the answer. The sincerity in his deep blue eyes makes me feel like I can trust him. I take another sip and decide I can give him an honest answer.

"My ex was a cop. He did some shit to me and when I went to the police, none of them did a damn thing." I know my voice has dropped a bit and I must have sounded weak. I instantly regret saying the words. I swallow and stare at my beer before taking a sip. It's the first time I'm actually talking about what happened and it's harder than I thought it'd be.

Blake's fists clench and he looks like he's going to flip the fucking bartop over. "What's his name?" His voice is hard and it comes out not so much as a question, but more as a demand. I flinch a little at his stern tone and obvious aggression. The grip on my beer tightens, but I try to calm myself down. He's not Vinny. Maddox and Pinch are quiet and still around me.

"It doesn't matter," I say and shake my head then give him a small smile. "It was a while ago."

He grabs my chin in his hand with his thumb running across my bottom lip and stares into my eyes. He's searching for something in my gaze and I'm not sure what, but he gives me a small, sad smile followed by a chaste kiss. It's a sweet gesture and I melt into his touch. When he leans back it's awkward with the sudden silence. I shift a little in my seat, wishing I hadn't said shit. Whatever. I take another swig. At least the beer is starting to taste better.

"What the hell do you need the police for anyway?" Maddox asks me with confusion on his face. I silently thank him for changing the subject. I don't want to talk about Vinny.

"Nothing, I was just telling Blake that if I did get into a situation like what it *looked* like out there, I wouldn't bother calling the cops." Maddox narrows his eyes and looks between me and Blake a few times.

Pinch just lets out a laugh, easing the bit of tension remaining. "If anyone tried to put their hand on you, I'm sure Blake would fuck 'em up. And then there's the rest of the club." He grabs a beer that the bartender holds out for him and pulls up the stool on my left side. "So don't worry about that, kitten."

"You too?" Blake asks all pissed off and looking like he wants to beat the shit out of something.

"What?" Pinch asks with all seriousness. Maddox lets out a deep laugh from his chest and puts his arm around my shoulders. I don't flinch at his playful touch. Instead I find myself leaning into his strong hold. He turns to Pinch, completely ignoring the angry stare from Blake.

"I think Blake is a little possessive of his hellcat." He gives Blake a huge grin. "He doesn't like it when we call her kitten."

Pinch lets out a high-pitched laugh. "That right, Blake?" Blake growls out an inaudible response which makes all three of us laugh and I can feel my skin heat with a blush. I'm starting to love that he's a bit possessive of me. It's addictive and I'm worried I'm going to be hooked.

"No, I don't fucking like it." He looks all butthurt again and I can't help but to push his buttons.

"I like it when you call me kitten, Pinch." I flirt a bit, softening my voice and lean toward Pinch while keeping a smartass grin on my face and eyeing Blake.

"That's the way you want to play, hellcat?" Blake

stands up from his seat and leans over me, forcing Maddox's arm to fall from my shoulder as Blake cages me in. His voice is low and threatening. His dominance forces a wave of desire through my body and my sore pussy clenches involuntarily. Both Pinch and Maddox are smiling like kids in a candy store. I bite my lip and nod my head while looking up at him through my dark, thick lashes.

"Yeah Blake, what're you gonna do about it?" I ask barely above a whisper.

Chapter 8

BLAKE

'M GOING TO SPANK HER ASS TILL SHE'S BEGGING me to fuck her. Maybe spank that tight pussy too. That's what I'm going to do about it. My dick throbs at the thought of getting her spread out in front of me. *Fuck, yes.* I'm going to give her a little preview upstairs and then I need to talk to Pinch real quick. As soon as that's done I'm taking her ass to my place. Just thinking about punishing that pussy has my dick straining against the zipper of my jeans. It takes every bit of restraint in me not to bend her ass over the bar and take her in front of everyone.

"Finish your beer," I whisper against her lips before giving her a bruising kiss. "Then I'm taking you up-stairs to show you what I'm going to do about it." When I lean back, the first thing I see is Pinch's goofy ass grin. He's a little gangly compared to the rest of us, but it fits his nerdy persona. "Hey Pinch, can I talk to you in the back room before I go?" I'm sure they already know why I'd want to talk to them. He nods, all the while grinning.

I grab my hellcat's beer and leave it on the bar. "See you guys in a bit." I don't wait for their response. Taking her hand, I lead her upstairs. This is gonna be quick, but so fucking good. I can hear her little pants as she struggles to keep up with me. I can't wait to have her begging and pleading for me to fuck her again. I grab my dick and readjust a little while I kick the door to my room shut. There's not much in here since I have an apartment not too far away, but there's a bed and privacy, which is all we need right now.

"Blake?" she asks nervously while scissoring her thighs together. She may not know what's going to happen, but she's sure as fuck turned on. I quickly take off all my clothes, all the while staring right at her.

"Yeah?"

"What are you gonna do?" She's throwing me a sexy as fuck look with her teeth sinking into her lower lip even as she fidgets with the hem of her dress.

I grin wickedly at her. "Get undressed." She

hesitates, so I add, "Don't make this any worse on yourself." She lets out a small gasp at my threat and starts unbuttoning her cardigan. I stroke my dick, watching her hands move.

"Pick up the pace." I don't need a striptease; I just want her bared to me. She leaves the sweater in a small pile on the floor and pulls that scrap of a dress over her head. I groan at the sight of her gorgeous body. She reaches down to unstrap her heels, but I stop her. "Leave them on and get on your knees. Now."

Her eyes never leave me as her lips part slightly, releasing a soft little moan, and she drops to her knees right in front of me. Her submission makes my dick that much harder.

"Open." Those pouty lips open wide and I waste no time slipping the head of my cock into her hot mouth. I pull back a little and she leans forward trying to keep her lips on it while her hands move to my thighs to catch her balance. *Little minx.*

"Uh uh," I say and she looks up at me as I admonish her behavior. "Hands behind your back." She does as she's told. I stroke my dick again and then lean down and run my fingers along her wet pussy. I sink two fingers into her heat and thumb her clit quickly. "Good girl." She moans at my touch and begins to clench around my fingers. I quickly remove them and stand back up, leaving her waiting for her release as I lick her juices off my fingers. Damn, her honey tastes even better than I imagined. I'll get my mouth on her pussy before we leave, I can guarantee that.

"Open wider." She looks at me like she's pissed that I didn't get her off, but I just stroke my dick with a cocky, lopsided grin on my face. She knows she's being punished. If she's smart, she'll take it like a good girl and get her reward after. I'm sure she's caught on to the plan, because she gives me a knowing look and opens her mouth wide for me.

"Smart choice, hellcat." I slide into her wet mouth and she obediently runs her hot tongue along the underside of my dick, flicking her tongue along the head. Marie covers her teeth with her lips and puts pressure down on my cock while hollowing her cheeks to suck more of me down her throat. With her eyes closed, moaning as my dick strokes in and out of her mouth, she's fucking gorgeous.

I grab the back of her head, holding her hair in my fists and plunge even deeper. She struggles to take me fully, but I hold her there until her throat closes around the tip of my dick. I pull all the way out and her eyes water as she gasps for air. It's a beautiful fucking sound. I smack my wet dick against her cheek and she turns her head to take me back in her mouth. *Fucking perfection.*

She bobs her head, sucking and moaning like it's the best fucking thing she's ever tasted. I start pumping mercilessly into her throat with short, shallow thrusts. I feel the telltale signs of my impending release as my balls draw up and tighten and I slam my dick down her throat and cum.

"Fuck!" I moan while watching for her reaction. She diligently swallows around my dick, milking more cum out of me. *Fuck yeah.* I love that she's enjoying this. How'd I get so fucking lucky? The base of my spine tingles as the last of my orgasm leaves me. She doesn't stop, licking at my slit, getting every last drop and sending a shiver down my back.

I don't hesitate to lift her up by her waist and throw her gorgeous ass on the bed. She's breathing heavy and still swallowing down my cum, but I don't care. I press my mouth to hers in a kiss and brutally shove my tongue in her mouth. She eagerly sucks my tongue and wraps her long legs around my hips, rubbing her hot pussy against my dick. It springs back to life instantly at the invitation of being inside her heat.

I break away from her mouth and move to her

neck, leaving bruising bites in my path down to her breasts. I want to mark her skin. I've wanted to do it since I saw her. I pinch one of her hard nipples and suck the other into my mouth; I bite down hard, making her buck against me and cry out in pleasure. I smile against her skin and stand up, leaving her on her back, legs parted on the bed. Waiting for me as her breathing calms down.

I stoke my hardening dick once again and ask, "You think I'm done punishing you, hellcat?" Her eyes pop open in shock and I laugh a bit then smack my hard dick against her clit over and over. Her thighs try to close at the intense pleasure, and I just smirk at her. I know that shit feels good. Her skin's flushed and her legs are shaking.

"Grab your knees and put your heels on the bed. I want you open for me." She does as I command, although her motions are slow and breathing ragged, and exposes her glistening pussy to me. Her chest rises and falls with desperation. I sink to my knees in front of her and drag my tongue along her hot cunt.

"Fuck, you taste so fucking sweet." I moan into her pussy and suck her throbbing clit. Her back arches as she throws her head back and lets out a strangled whimper.

"Please, Blake." A deep chuckle leaves my chest. I lift my head and wait for her to meet my gaze.

When her eyes reach mine, I ask, "Please what, hellcat?"

She begs in a whisper, "Please make me cum."

I tsk and wait a few agonizing seconds, holding her gaze. "You really shouldn't try to make me jealous." She parts her lips to respond, but stops when I push two thick fingers deep into her wet sex and stroke the rough patch at her front wall. She thrashes on the bed as her body starts to tremble and I have to hold her firmly in place to keep her where I want her. I feel her pussy start to clamp down on my fingers and just as her orgasm approaches, I stop and take out my fingers to suck on them.

My little spitfire practically hisses at me, "Blake!" I chuckle at how pissed she is. I lower my head again and lap at her swollen nub.

"This what you want?" She moans and grabs my head with both her hands, digging her nails into my scalp. She's trying to use my tongue for her plea-sure and I'm going to put a stop to that right now. Tonight she can use my face all she wants. But right now, nope. Not going to fucking happen. She needs to be punished.

I pull back, breaking her hold on me and growl at her, "You going to make me tie you up?" She's practically gasping for air as she shakes her head. "Good girl, now put your hands above your head and leave them there." She immediately obeys, frantic for her orgasm. Before feasting on her cunt again, I push my fingers back in her pussy to get them soaked with her honey. "You ever been fucked in your ass, hellcat?" Her whole body tenses, giving me the answer I need.

She nervously replies, "No."

"I'm going to get you ready for tonight, just relax." I lick her from her puckered hole all the way to her clit. When I get to that swollen nub I suck it in quickly, and it makes a popping noise when I pull back. At the same time, I push one finger up to the knuckle into her ass. She gasps and bears down on my finger.

"Relax, I got you." I almost call her kitten. The nickname almost slips from my lips. After a few licks at her throbbing clit, I feel the tension release and I start moving in, slowly slipping more of my finger into her tight hole. I lick her again before tongue fucking her pussy.

"Yes!" She screams out and almost grabs my head again. I pull back to scold her, but she quickly realizes her mistake and puts her hands back into position. I wait a moment, watching her hands before I go back to work. Her pussy is fucking sweet and I could eat it all night, but I have to meet up with Pinch before I take her home. And I really want to fuck her on my bed as soon as fucking possible.

I push my finger in and out, prepping her ass. I lap at her nub again before sucking it into my mouth gently. She moans into her arm to muffle the sound. I slip another finger in and start tongue fucking her again. It's fucking tight, but both my middle and pointer finger fit. *Thank fuck.* For a minute I was worried I wasn't going to be able to get into that ass tonight. My hard dick twitches at the thought.

Her body starts to shake again and she's struggling to hold still. She's close. She moans and her pussy clamps down on my tongue. And that's where I'm going to leave her.

I withdraw my fingers and stand up. My dick is still hard as fuck, but I'm going to have to wait, just like my little hellcat. I reach for my jeans after cleaning up and take a look at her flushed, delectable body. I smile at the hickey I left on her breast. My claim on her. She jackknifes on the bed at the realization that I'm leaving.

"What're you doing?" she asks with her chest

heaving. My eyes immediately go to her hardened, pink nipples. I almost groan at the sight. I can't fucking wait to suck on them tonight.

"I have to go talk to Pinch and then I'm taking you home."

"But-" I cut her off before she can finish.

"I told you. You shouldn't have made me jealous, hellcat." She looks like she's going to beat the shit out of me, but instead she moves to sit cross-legged on the bed and pulls the comforter around her, avoiding eye contact. I grab her dress and lean down to give it to her. She snatches it out of my hand and I chuckle before giving her a small peck on the cheek, which she pulls away from. She looks ready to rip my fucking face off, so I don't risk going in for a kiss on the lips.

"Don't push me, hellcat." She looks up through her lashes at me with a scowl on her face.

"Now give me a kiss before I go and when I take you home, I'll take care of you." She purses her lips before leaning up to give me too quick of a peck. Her lips barely fucking touched mine. For a moment I second-guess what I'm doing. She's really fucking pissed that I didn't get her off. It'll be that much better for her later though. I nod my head at the thought. Yeah, waiting will only add to her pleasure. I'll let her ride my tongue and use my face for her pleasure. She'll fucking love me then.

"Don't touch yourself." I look at her hard and narrow my eyes. I'm not stupid. She'd get herself off the second I leave this room if I hadn't told her not to. She crosses her arms across her chest and looks at me like I'm a goddamn villain.

"I'll meet you at the bar in a few minutes," I tell her. She doesn't make eye contact, instead just nodding her head. I hesitate, but decide to leave. She'll be alright. She just has to learn not to make me jealous. I'm sure that taught her a fucking lesson.

MARIE

That fucking asshole! As soon as he closes the door, I collapse back onto the bed and cover my face with my hands. My emotions are off the chart. It's so fucking hard not to cry right now. That cocky bastard used me for his pleasure like I was just some whore.

Yeah I fucking enjoyed it at the time, but right now it fucking hurts. A sob rocks through my body and I let it. The tears start pouring down my face. I feel so degraded. Had he let me cum and held me afterward, I wouldn't be feeling like this. But he used me to get off, then teased me and left. The sobs grow more intense and I gasp for breath. I'm not going to lie here and fucking cry over this bullshit. I wipe angrily under my eyes and slowly get off the bed.

There's a mirror on the dresser and I move to it to fix myself. My skin's flushed and a bit of mascara is running, but I clean it up the best I can. The only evidence that I cried are my red-rimmed eyes. I close them and press my palms against the lids. I let my body calm for a few minutes before grabbing my cardigan. I breathe out deep and will myself to calm the fuck down.

I'm struggling with what to do. I fucking loved what happened, but hated that he left me here and even worse, that he didn't let me cum. *Bastard.* I stare at myself in the mirror. That's one fucked up way to get back at someone.

Maybe I'll fuck with him tonight. I smile in the mirror, feeling like a badass bitch again. Yeah he humiliated me, but I fucking loved it. I button up my cardigan and take a deep breath to head back downstairs. I've got to think of some way to get that fucker back. As I walk down the stairs, I have to stifle back a moan. I'm so damn close. Part of me wants to get myself off. It wouldn't take much, just a few hard strokes against my clit. I moan when I remember him smacking my clit with his dick. A shudder of pleasure runs through my body. That felt so fucking good. I'll play his game. Even if he's a bastard.

As I get to the landing and head into the main room, a pretty little blonde twig bumps into me.

"Oh shit, sorry." I bite my lip and step back. "My bad." She smiles and waves her hand.

"No, it was my fault. I'm sorry." I smile back and start to move past her toward the bar, but she puts her hand on my arm to stop me.

"Did you go up there with Blake?" *Why the fuck does she want to know?* I narrow my eyes at her.

"Yeah, he just came down a second ago. Were you heading up there to talk to him or something?" She laughs at my question.

"Yeah, sure. Or something." She laughs again. "But seriously, are you done with him? I was really hoping to get into his bed again tonight." My breath leaves my body.

Into his bed.

Again.

The tears threaten to come back, but I will them away.

It shouldn't hurt this bad. Why does that hurt so much? It's because I'm stupid, that's why.

She looks oblivious. Like her words wouldn't fucking hurt. Like this kind of shit is normal. Maybe it is normal for her. *And Blake.* What the hell was I thinking?

"Yeah, I'm done with him." I force a small smile. "Do you have a phone I can use?"

She smiles brightly back at me.

"Yeah, sure!" She reaches into her back pocket and hands me an outdated flip phone. I call the only number I know by heart other than my own.

"Hello?" Lexi's voice answers on the second ring, sounding worried.

"Lexi-" As soon as I say her name, she shrieks into the phone.

"Oh my God, Marie! Where the hell are you? I'm out of my fucking mind over here!"

I roll my eyes at her outburst. *Yeah, okay Lexi.*

"Are you at the bar?" I don't have time to fuck around. The blonde twig is watching me and I'm pretty sure she's trying to listen in on the conversation.

"Yeah I got here-" she starts to say, but I cut her off. At this point I can tell I'm not going to be able to stop the damn tears from coming and I just need to get the hell out of here.

"I'm down the street, a few blocks toward the train station. Can you meet me at the corner?"

"Yeah. Are you okay?" The hysteria has gone down a notch and she's obviously concerned. The tears well and I take a deep breath.

"Yeah, just come get me please."

Chapter 9

BLAKE

HEAD TO THE BACK ROOM WHERE THE MEETINGS take place, leaving Marie upstairs. I can't wait to get in that ass tonight. I'll get her off first. At least once. I smile and lick my lower lip. I can still taste her on my tongue. *Fucking delicious.* She'll be fine while I talk to Pinch. She's safe here. And she fits right in.

Damn, I wish I'd just asked her if she wanted me to walk her home, so we could've started this off without any lying. But then again, I never would've let them think she was my girl. No way in hell I'd ever have brought her in here. My smile vanishes. She's only safe while I'm safe. Shit, things are a little more fucked than I'd like them to be at this point. But I'll be damned if I'm not keeping her. I want her more than anything. Every protective instinct in me is on high alert. I don't know what it is about her, but my body is begging me to claim her. And I'm hard-pressed not to listen.

I barge into the meeting room without knocking. No need to, since I knew they'd be in here waiting for me. And now that I'm back here, I'm all pissed off again. That fucker messed with my hellcat. I meet Maddox with a hard glare.

"Calm down, Blake." He stares me down as I lean against the desk. "You can't go shooting her ex-boyfriend. He's a cop."

"I'm not going to shoot him." Not to kill, anyway. Pinch closes the door so it's just the three of us.

"Blake," he starts as though he's warning me, asking me to back off, but he won't make me. Maddox will let me have this if I want it. And God, do I want it. No one's going to hurt my hellcat and get away with it.

"You telling me you're not just as pissed as I am that her ex got away with … " I can't finish. Fuck! I don't even know what the hell he did exactly, but I'm going to find out. I'm going to find out tonight. After I get her under me.

"Already a step ahead of you," Pinch chimes in and

holds up her ID. He goes over to the computer and starts plugging in her info.

"You swiped her ID?" Pinch never fails to surprise me. A pickpocket and hacker, he's a thief in every sense of the word.

He turns in his chair and looks back at me like he doesn't see a problem with it. "Well, yeah. It's not like you'd know her last name." No I don't, but he didn't know that. I glare at him and he shakes his head. "Okay then, what's her last name?" *Fucking asshole.*

I let out a small growl and say, "Just do what you have to do."

"So, how are you planning to handle this?" Maddox's starting in on me again.

"You remember that prick who hit your sister?" I stare straight back at him, meeting his hard glower. "You didn't have a problem knocking his teeth in."

"He wasn't a cop."

"Since when does that matter?" I shouldn't be talking back, but I'm furious. I'm so fucking pissed that someone put their hands on Marie. And even angrier that no one helped her. No one was there for her. But I'm here now.

An uncomfortable moment passes before he lets out a loud exhale. "You want help?" he asks like I'm a huge pain in his ass. I pat him on the back in thanks, but shake my head.

"Naw, just get me his address."

"Got it. You're gonna want to give his name to Linc though, so he can ask his contacts at the PD for his schedule." I nod my head calmly, but my gut churns at his words. When I first found out they were paying people off at the PD, I freaked the fuck out. Roger told me he knew all of Linc's contacts and I was safe. I can't fucking take doing this anymore. I could be their contact. But it's too late for that now. I fucking wish it wasn't. They're the only family I have. Pinch prints something off and then hands me a piece of paper with the prick's information.

"Don't worry," I say and look at Maddox, "I'll be discreet." I turn to leave them while folding the paper, but Maddox's hand comes down hard on my shoulder. I look back, waiting for him to say something, but he just stares at me.

"Yeah?" The question leaves my mouth after a moment of silence.

He's holding something back, so I turn to fully face him. "What's on your mind, brother?" Something's wrong and I don't fucking like it. I glance at Pinch. He's grinning like he always does. My gaze falls back on Maddox. His jaw's tense; he's working too hard not to say whatever's on his mind. "Just let it out."

He hesitates before asking, "Were you two really just playing around?"

My blood runs cold at the question. I square my shoulders as I feel something shift between us. I stare back at him and keep eye contact while I shake my head. "No." I can't fucking lie to him. I'm exhausted from the lies. I just want to get everything off my chest. All of it.

"You lied to me." It's a statement, not a question.

I nod my head once and reply in a clipped tone, "Yup." The room's silent for what feels like forever. Both of us just glaring at each other with clenched fists, waiting for the other to make their move. "You want to ask me anything else, Maddox?" I may as well give it to him. I'm tired of waiting for it all to come crashing down. I can hear my blood rushing into my ears and my heart's pounding in my chest. *Just ask me.* Minutes tick by and he finally gives it to me.

"You a cop, Blake?"

I don't even hesitate while I look him right in the eyes and reply, "Yeah, I am." As the words leave my mouth, the printer goes off next to me, making both of us jump.

"Here you go." Pinch turns in the chair and hands me a piece of paper before glancing down to my hands and saying, "You ripped that one to shreds, so I figured you'd want a new one." He gives me a huge grin and shrugs as he casually adds, "We already knew."

What the fuck? I feel like he punched me in the gut. I turn to Maddox, seeing nothing but red and ask, "You knew?"

"Yeah." He doesn't change his emotionless expression in the least. "Since day one." *Motherfucker!* I clench my fists, ready to punch this fucker right in his smug face.

"All those times I tried to fucking tell you, and you cut me off." To say I'm pissed off would be a massive understatement. I've shared everything with him, everything I went through overseas, and then the shit I came home to. I wanted to tell him every fucking day since we put his old man in the ground, but he kept shutting me down. That motherfucker.

"You have some fucking nerve to be pissed at me!" He puts his face less than an inch away from mine, invading my space and egging me on. "You're the fucking cop!"

Pinch gets between us and shoves Maddox hard in his chest. He may be gangly, but he's fucking lethal.

Maddox's hard body slams into the back wall. "Shut your fucking mouth, Maddox. They'll hear you." I'm suddenly acutely aware of the fact that we're in the clubhouse and I've just admitted to being a cop.

My thoughts fly to Marie. My stomach drops and I start cracking each knuckle on my fists. "Marie's got nothing to do with any of this shit." I have to clear her. "Fuck, I just met her tonight. I fucking swear it."

"We know," Pinch pipes up. Relief floods through me.

"Who else knows?"

Pinch answers with his typical ease and his grin returns as he sits back down. "Just the two of us and Pres. And Jace."

I snort. "Of course Jace knows. He's always following me around like a lost puppy and spouting off shit about the shipments."

"You tell your boss about the shipments?" Maddox's eyeing me like an asshole.

"The Pres is my boss." The words come out hard, daring him to contradict me. I haven't had a real conversation with Roger in months. Not only that, but there's nothing to say about the shipments. They control the port, but I've never seen anything shady come through. Shit ton of pot, but that's not worth mentioning.

"Stop fucking with him." Pinch looks at me after telling Maddox off. "We know you don't say shit about the shipments. Roger's the one who sent you to us." *This just keeps getting better and better.* He smiles like a lunatic then says, "And he's the PD contact."

My whole body feels like it's shaking with rage. "You know how hard it was for me to go through with everything last week?" I glare at Maddox. "Why'd you fucking cut me off? You had to know this is what I was getting at." I felt like a fraud. And like a pussy for not telling them. The guys are my family. I'd done everything I could to prove it to them, but with that shit weighing on me, it just didn't feel right getting patched. Maddox stares at me for the longest fucking time. So long, I don't think he's going to answer me.

"I don't like the fact that you're a cop." He shrugs, and for the first time since I admitted the truth, he relaxes a bit. "It was easier to just pretend you weren't."

"Now what?" I have to ask. "You guys going to kill me?"

"What the fuck, Blake?" Pinch looks at me like I kicked his puppy. Even Maddox takes a step back and side-eyes me like I'm the crazy one.

"Well, what the hell am I supposed to think?" My anger has taken over. I'm running on pure adrenaline and anxiety.

"Think of it like a job interview, only we didn't want you to realize you were applying."

"It took you two fucking years to figure out that you wanted me for the job?" The question rips up my throat with outrage.

"Well technically we wanted to patch you last year, but Pres liked fucking with you or something and you didn't seem like you were in a rush."

"Why didn't he tell me before last week?" It fucking hurts. I can't help it. I wanted to be patched, but not as a fucking undercover cop. My rage fades as I realize what a blow it was for them to know and not tell me.

Pinch shrugs. "Maybe he wanted to see if you'd tell him."

"Shit." If that's the case, then I failed him. I'm not as close to Linc as I am with Maddox. In fact, I've kept a lot of shit that the two of us have gotten into from Linc. Now it's just guilt eating at me. I've got to talk to Linc, ASAP.

"What about the chick?" Pinch's question makes my fists clench and my blood run cold.

"What about her?" I can't help the growl that escapes.

"Well, you making her your old lady?" His question lifts a fucking ton of weight off my shoulders. I almost smile. Almost.

"If I'd known her more than a few hours, I'd be able to answer that. For now, just keep your hands off."

Pinch lets out his signature, high-pitched laugh looking crazy as fuck and Maddox shakes his head, making the ghost of a smile on my face vanish. His lips are pressed in a hard line. He hasn't looked at me like that since I first came to the club. I feel like I failed him.

"We good?" I ask him in all seriousness. I don't know what I'd do if I lost him. The thought makes my chest feel hollow.

"Yeah." His hard eyes soften and he grabs me in a bear hug. I pat him hard on the back. *Thank fuck.*

"I'm fucking sorry."

"Me too, brother." He grabs the piece of paper in my hands. "You sure you don't want help fucking this guy up?" A grin spreads across my face.

"I guess I could use some help."

"Go take your hellcat home and let me know where to meet you."

I shake out my shoulders and nod at the guys,

leaving the back room feeling like I can breathe easy. The weight that's been holding me down for years has finally been lifted. I still need to talk to Linc though. Guilt starts to creep up again, but I push it aside. I'll take care of Marie first.

I search the bar for her, but she's not there. I grab my barstool and wait for her to come back from the bathroom, figuring that must be where she went. After a few minutes pass, I start to get up thinking she must be upstairs still, but Tammy sidles up next to me, halting my movement.

"Whatcha doing tonight, Blake?" Her flirtatious tone is unwelcome. She knows damn well I'm here with Marie. I noticeably lean away from her; if my hellcat comes back down and sees me with Tammy, I don't know what she'll think. Hopefully the way I'm sitting will make it obvious that I'm not interested. To both of them.

"I came here with my girl."

Tammy's a pretty little thing, but she just wants to be on the arm of any of the members. I don't have any problems letting her down easy.

"I know, but she just left."

I stare at her and my brow furrows in confusion

and disbelief. "What?" I look around the main room, searching for her gorgeous ass.

"Yeah, she asked to use my phone and took off." She says the words easily and leans closer to me, putting her hand on my thigh. I push her off the second her hand hits me. She protests, looking wounded by my rejection, but I don't give a fuck.

She fucking left me? I try to swallow down the lump forming in my throat. I really thought we had something. My fist slams on the bar. I fucking know we had something special between us. It's my own damn fault. I pushed her too hard, too fast. It's the way I've always been. Fuck! I finally got everything straightened out with the MC and the same fucking night, she leaves me. I've got to get her back. I'm not going to let her go without fighting for her.

I ignore Tammy and whatever words are falling out of her mouth, and walk with long, powerful strides to the back room. Pinch and Maddox are still there, relaxed around the computer and looking at some video online. When they see my face, both of them look back with concern and Maddox shoots up from his spot ready to take out whoever I need him to.

"She took off."

The confidence leaves Maddox's face. He's never

kept a girl, so he wouldn't know what the hell to do. Neither have I.

"What'd you do to scare her off?"

I shake my head. I know I was pushing her limits, but I thought she could take it. I thought she fucking loved it. I feel like a piece of shit.

I'm pissed that she left. I'm pissed she didn't tell me she wasn't happy. I'm pissed that I pushed her too hard. To be honest, I'm just pissed the fuck off. "I just need her address." I stare pointedly at Pinch. "Where's that ID?"

"What'd you do to our kitten, Blake?" Maddox interjects.

"She's not *our* kitten. She's mine." Maddox huffs at my words; his nostrils flare and his fists clench. I can see the wheels turning in his head as the silence settles in between us.

"Maybe if she was *ours*, she wouldn't have left you," he points out easily and I fucking lose it. The last thread holding me together snaps. I've been on edge all night and this just breaks something in me.

Adrenaline pumps through my body, burning up my skin. I hear the loud, pulsing thud of my blood in my ears. A snarl rips through me as I slam both of my fists into Maddox's shoulders, landing hard and knocking into him with all my weight. He stumbles, smashing his shoulder and head against the brick wall. Before he gains his balance, I land a blow into his gut that nearly has him doubling over. But Maddox's a huge fucker who's taken enough punches to know how to handle them. He mutters under his breath, "Stupid fuck!" while ramming his shoulder into my gut. My legs lose their balance as my boot backs into the fucking rug, tripping me.

I fall hard on my ass and elbows with Maddox's large frame crushing down on mine. I quickly wrap a leg around his calf and push my weight to the opposite shoulder, forcing him down on his back with me landing hard on his chest. My fist slams into the floor as I try to gain my balance and focus. It hurts like a bitch as I get up clenching my fists and the movement splits my knuckles. My left hand grabs the collar of his shirt as I raise my bloodied right fist. But before I'm able to gain my balance and take a swing at him, he plants a punch on my left cheek. *Fuck!* I stagger back, both fists immediately going to my face to block any more punches. I land on my ass, but move to my feet the second I see Maddox breathing heavy and struggling to get up.

"What the fuck are you two going at it for?"

Linc's words barely register as my fist connects with Maddox's hard jaw. My knuckles scream at the contact and pain shoots up my arm before running back down to my aching fist. Fuck, that hurt. Maddox's got a hand cradling that side of his face and he's rubbing his jaw. At least it fucking hurt him too.

"Maddox wants to fuck my girl. He doesn't fucking understand that she's mine."

"Fuck you. You may have seen her first, but that doesn't make her yours."

"Shut the fuck up. Both of you. You two want to tear each other apart, fine by me. Fight it out in the ring tomorrow." A moment passes of silence. All I can hear is the blood still roaring in my ears and our heavy breathing. I glare at Maddox before facing Linc.

The second I see him, all I can think about is how he brought me on, even knowing I was undercover. How he patched me, knowing I was a cop. He has no idea I know. It feels like everything is crumbling around me. Fuck. My girl left me, the only girl I ever fucking wanted. My best friend wants to sleep with her. And the only people I ever considered family have known for years that I've been lying to them.

Something hard drops in the pit of my stomach as my heart lurches in my chest.

I open my mouth, but the words don't come out. I slam my mouth shut and clench my fists, wanting to beat the shit out of Maddox all over again. Anything to get rid of this pain pushing down on me. I don't know how to tell Linc. How the hell do I tell him? My blood runs cold and all I can hear is a pounding in my ears.

I hear Maddox spit in the trashcan before he says, "Blake's got some prick's info for Roger, Pres." I glance over at him and he gives me a tight smile. I give the same tense smile back and relax my fists. Even after knocking him around, he's still helping me out.

It takes a minute for Linc to register what Maddox just told him. I see the moment it finally clicks, because his face lights up and a smile takes over his face; a rough chuckle barrels through his chest. "Well, it's about damn time." His left hand comes down on my shoulder and squeezes before he grabs me in a bear hug. *What the fuck?* "Who told you?"

Pinch pipes up before I can respond and says,

"Maddox was fucking around with him, Pres. So I told him."

Linc's smile slips. "What do you mean?" Before anyone can answer he adds, "Who told you we knew you were a cop?" I feel my forehead pinch in confusion. Why the fuck does it matter? I'm not going to question Linc though. You don't question Pres.

"I did." Pinch looks curious too. His normal smile has faded and his eyes are darting between the three of us. I've rarely seen him anything other than happy as a pig in shit, so seeing him eyeing the fuck out of everyone is making my own nerves race through me.

"Damn it, Pinch!" Pinch cringes at Linc's outburst. "You cost me twenty grand." Linc starts shaking his head before smacking Maddox on the back of his. We all flinch at the sound, because it sure as hell wasn't a love tap, and Maddox takes a step closer to me. As if I can protect him from Pres if it comes to that.

"What the hell's wrong with you, Maddox?" Linc's hard eyes bore into Maddox's as he asks, "He's the closest thing you've got to family, and you didn't tell him?"

It's easy to see Maddox's confusion on his face.

He parts his lips to respond, but nothing comes out. His eyes shift hesitantly to me and then back to Linc's before he points out, "Pres, you told me not to."

"I told you not to do a lot of shit, but that didn't stop you two, did it?" I press my lips into a hard, tight line waiting for Maddox to respond. How does he know about that? And what exactly does he know? I'm not admitting shit.

He clenches his fists and opens his mouth, but nothing comes out. His eyes find mine and I shake my head slowly, silently telling him that I didn't tell Linc anything.

Linc rubs his hands down his face and mutters, "Dammit Maddox, you owe me twenty grand." He shakes his head one last time and looks at the two of us like we've disappointed him.

"You two get your shit settled. But if you wanna fight it out, you do it in the ring. I have to call Roger." Link slams the door shut on his way out, cursing us under his breath.

The three of us stare at the closed door.

"That's why he didn't tell me?" I look between the two of them slowly. "Because of a bet?"

"Who the fuck would bet twenty grand on that?" Pinch's brows are knitted and he runs his hand through his hair in confusion while sitting back in his seat. Silence settles over the room.

"You know I meant what I said earlier." Maddox's voice breaks the quiet.

"Which part of what you said?" For the life of me, I don't know what he's getting at. But if it's about Marie, we're gonna have problems.

"Maybe between the two of us, we can keep her." Motherfucker just won't let it go.

"Don't make me kill you, Maddox."

He holds up both hands in surrender, but refuses to shut the fuck up. "Just listen to me." I shake my head and curl my lip as rage pumps through me. "I know she's not just a piece of ass." His words make me pause, but only for a second.

"You think she's going to listen to you when you show up at her place?" My eyes dart to the floor for a split second in doubt before meeting his.

"You think she'd listen to you? But not me?" I sneer and resist the urge to spit.

"Calm the fuck down, Blake."

"Fuck you! You're trying to take her from me!"

"I'm not taking anything from you. I want to share her." My hands tighten into fists, making my split knuckles scream in agony. I tilt my head and crack my neck. My body's on edge and I want nothing more than to take out all this pent-up energy on Maddox's face.

"I wouldn't know what the fuck to do with a girl like Marie. But I want her. I can't help it."

"Maddox, I'm warning you." My low voice is steady, the threat dripping with menace. Marie's not some fling. I want more from her. More *with* her.

"I can help you. We can be everything she wants." My nostrils flare in anger, but deep down that fucking hurt.

"You think she won't want me? Is that it? I'm not good enough for her?" His words gut me, taking advantage of my insecurities.

"I didn't fucking say that." Maddox's face flashes with remorse before taking on a hard edge. "That's not what I meant, and you know it."

"What the fuck did you mean?"

"I want her. I *want* her." He pauses, his eyes searching mine, pleading with me to understand him. "Not just as a piece of ass, but to keep. I know you want her too. Between the two of us, she'll stay." I turn my back to him to face the door, letting his words settle. Maddox continues talking to my back.

"I know she will. You'll fuck up and I'll fuck up, but one of us will always be there to keep her."

"I want her, Maddox." I finally turn back to him. "I don't know if I can keep her, but I want to."

"I know you do; I do too."

I nod my head at him. "I fucked up. I know I did." I breathe out deep and say, "I don't know if I wanna share her." I shake my head and admit, "I don't want to scare her off."

"Let me go with you." He takes a step forward. "I think she wants it."

I quirk a brow at him. "Why do you think that?"

He shrugs his shoulders. "It won't hurt to see, right? If I'm wrong, I'll back off."

I consider what he's saying. Obviously I'm doing a shit job of keeping her if I can't even hold onto her for one night. We've shared women before and they fucking loved it. This will be different obviously, since we don't want to let her go. "You really think we can keep her?"

He grins back at me as he says, "Hell yeah! I know we can make our kitten happy." He rubs his jaw and says, "You got me pretty good."

An asymmetric smile pulls on my lips as I point out, "You fucking had it coming."

He belts out a deep laugh.

"I swear to God if this scares her off, I'm taking you in the ring tomorrow."

"It's not gonna fucking happen. Marie's gonna be rubbing our shoulders while we fuck up the Rogue MC."

"Bunch of pussies." I shake out my shoulders and suck the blood off one of my knuckles. "I probably shouldn't have hit you."

He shrugs again and then gives me a devilish grin. "Probably not. Your face looks like shit."

Chapter 10

MARIE

"WHAT THE FUCK HAPPENED TO YOUR neck?" Lexi stares at me from her seat behind the wheel, mouth open in shock. "Blake happened to my neck. He's a fucking prick." Tears are still lingering in my eyes. I ran out of the clubhouse as fast as I could and waited on the corner for her, feeling like a cheap hooker. The cold, fresh air helped calm me down though.

"What happened? Are you alright?" I shake my head. I'm so fucking stupid. It's been a year since I split from Vinny. I finally decide to sleep with someone and it has to be a biker who probably won't even care that I'm gone. I cover the marks on my neck with my hand and stare out into the night. He's probably already in bed with that blonde. I hope that bitch doesn't let him cum. I snort at the thought.

Whatever.

I'm not that kind of girl anyway. I'm not the girl that hooks up with a biker, gets nailed in public and dreams of threesomes with his sexy friend. Well, tonight I might have been that kind of girl. But it's over. My stupid heart clenches, wishing it wasn't.

"I decided to get laid and now I regret it." I look straight ahead as she goes right through a stop sign. She didn't even try to brake. "What the fuck, Lexi?"

"What?" She stares at me with wide eyes, not paying an ounce of attention to the road.

"Eyes on the road! You blew through that stop sign!"

"Oh shit." She lifts her ass up to look in the rearview mirror. Probably checking for cops. I gape at her. "Whatever, it's not like we're gonna get pulled over."

"What the hell is wrong with you tonight? You don't show up? You don't answer my texts? You're driving like a fucking maniac!"

"Sorry." She runs her hands through her hair, taking both off the wheel for a second too fucking long. She grips the wheel and looks out her window before taking a deep breath and looking straight ahead. Her voice lowers and a sad frown pulls her pouty lips down as she says, "It's just been a fucked up day." Her response softens my heart and suddenly I don't give a shit about anything other than what's got her looking so upset.

"What happened?" I feel a need to protect her. Lexi's naïve and gets her heart hurt a lot. I have a bad feeling her day's gone to shit because of her ass of an ex. She purses her lips and shakes her head before wiping stray tears from her eyes with the palm of her hand.

"I don't wanna talk about it."

I put a consoling hand on her thigh and squeeze lightly. "It's alright, babe."

"I'm sorry I'm such a shit friend." She gasps for air in between sobs. Fuck. She should really pull over.

"It's alright. It's okay. You want me to drive?" I keep my voice soft even though her driving is really starting to freak me out. She shakes her head and breathes in deep, trying to calm herself down. I sit back in my seat and look out the window; we're a few minutes away from her place and I can just walk home from there. I'm only a block down from her.

"You remember when Friday nights used to be so much fun for us?" She nods her head and smiles. "When did we get to be so lame?"

She snorts, "You just got laid by a biker and you think that's lame?" I laugh without humor and without warning the tears come back.

"I'm so fucking stupid." My head slams into the headrest as I slump in the seat. "I really thought there was something between us."

"Was it just a good time for him?"

I wipe the bastard tears with the back of my hand and sniffle while I nod my head. "Yeah. One of many, I guess."

"You going to be alright tonight?" I know what she's getting at, and it's nice of her to ask, but I'd rather be alone tonight. I turn in my seat to tell her that I'm going to bed with a bottle of wine, but the look on her face makes me think she needs me.

"You want me to stay with you?" I offer. I may not want company, but it looks like she does. She shakes her head at my question though.

"Not if you don't want company. I need to be alone." I don't think the last part was for me, but I nod my head anyway.

"Your tattooed hunk was there tonight." I shift

110

in the seat, adjusting my dress, and keep my eyes on her, gauging her reaction. The mention of her crush does nothing to brighten her spirits.

She noticeably swallows before muttering, "He must have left before I got there."

I pout and say, "Sorry." Damn, I didn't mean to make her feel any worse. I slink back in my seat and I see that we're pulling up to my place.

She shakes her head. "Don't be. I only went to find you when I realized your phone was dead."

"You didn't have to drop me off; I could've walked."

"Yeah I did." She looks at me with sad eyes and a small smile. "I'm sorry I left you hanging tonight." I lean over the console and give her a firm hug. I hold on a second longer than usual.

"It's alright, babe," I say and look deep into her blue eyes, "everything's gonna be alright." She widens her sad smile.

"Love you, girl." She gives me a small kiss on the cheek and I do the same.

"Love you too."

I climb out of her car exhausted, sore and feeling beat up from head to toe. The trek up the two flights of stairs to my apartment takes every bit of energy that I have. I dig in my clutch for my keys as I climb up the last few steps while letting all of my tension out in a bitter sigh. I should've known better. I swallow the lump in my throat and nearly trip on the last stair when I look up from my clutch. Blake's standing outside my apartment.

He's holding a leather jacket in his right hand while leaning his back against my door. A white t-shirt is stretched tight across his chiseled chest and that tattoo running from his neck down his arm is on full display. Standing next to him with his corded, muscular arms crossed is Maddox. The two of them stare back at me with small grins playing on their gorgeous faces. My heart leaps up my throat, suffocating me. The chill leaves my skin as my body heats up and my blood starts pumping with desire.

I part my lips to speak but Blake kicks off the door and strides toward me. He's so fucking intimidating, I almost take a step back.

"Uh uh, my little hellcat." His arm wraps around my shoulders before slowly slipping to my waist as he walks me to my door. "If you thought you were in trouble before, you're in for one hell of a surprise."

"You should've known better than to take off,

kitten," Maddox reprimands me before taking my key from my hand and unlocking my door.

BLAKE

I'm not sure if she's scared or turned on. She keeps eyeing Maddox and me and twisting her fingers together before staring at the floor then back up to us. We walk her in and thank God she doesn't fight us. I didn't know what we'd be up against when we got here.

"What are you guys doing here?" she finally speaks in a breathy voice, looking between the two of us as I shut the door.

Her apartment's nothing like what I expected. I knew she was classy because of the way she carried herself, but damn, she must be loaded. The place looks like a picture from a magazine. Everything is clean and organized. Shit, I thought I'd have a hard time keeping her before we got here. Seeing her place, I know I'm going to have a hard time keeping her sweet ass. Maddox strides in and grabs a bottle of wine from her kitchen like he's done it a thousand times before. I take a page from his book and push my insecurities down, plastering a cocky grin on my face.

"Well, since you left in a hurry, I figured you wanted to finish up at your place, not mine."

Something in her bristles at my arrogant attitude. "Figured you'd be banging that blonde chick." She huffs to the kitchen, slamming her clutch down on the counter and snatches the bottle from Maddox's hand. "I'm not fucking disposable. Yeah I fucked you and I loved it, but I'm not that kind of girl."

"What the hell are you talking about?" Maddox's hard voice doesn't even startle her as he yanks the bottle back and opens up a drawer before closing it and then opening up the next.

"What blonde?" I feel my brows knit together in confusion. "I thought you were pissed because I didn't let you cum."

She huffs at Maddox and opens up a drawer on the far left before handing him a bottle opener. "You could ask." She sneers at Maddox before looking back at me with hurt written all over her gorgeous face. "The blonde who you slept with before. What's the matter? You can't keep them straight?"

"Watch your mouth, hellcat. I don't fuck around. Not like what you're thinking anyway. Are you talking about Tammy?"

"I don't know what her name is. Skinny blonde who said she was getting into your bed *again* tonight."

She's really pissed off, but I'm not going to take that lip from her.

"I told you to watch your mouth. I didn't fuck Tammy or any of the other women that were there tonight." I take a chance and lean down to leave a bruising kiss on her pouty lips. She takes a step back and bumps into the counter. I put one hand on either side of her, caging her in. "And I sure as shit know you're not disposable. That's why we're here." She parts those swollen cherry lips and looks to her left at Maddox, who's busy pouring the wine into three glasses, as if we drink wine, and then back to me.

I can tell she's softening, so I lean down and rub my nose against hers. "Is that why you left me? You weren't mad about what I did?" Her eyes widen and the anger vanishes, replaced with a look of regret.

"I was mad about how you left me," she says and shuffles her feet a bit, looking anywhere but in my eyes. I grab her chin with my thumb resting on her bottom lip and tilt her face to look at mine.

"I'm sorry I left you like I did."

Maddox interrupts our little moment, but I don't mind. "What'd Blake do to you, kitten?" His rough voice makes Marie jump and I notice her small gasp as she clenches her thighs. The two of us smirk. How did I not realize that she was into him? Maybe Maddox was right. Knowing she left because of Tammy pisses me off, but more than that, it makes me hopeful.

She eyes me questioningly before looking back at Maddox. I keep my face impassive. If she wants to tell him, she can. If not, I'll take that as a sign that we're wrong and she doesn't want both of us. But she better still want me.

"He," her eyes glance back at mine before staring straight at Maddox, "he didn't let me … cum."

He hands her a glass of wine, which she takes with both of hers. "Why'd he do that?"

"He was punishing me for flirting with Pinch." The words fall off her lips easily, like he has her in some sort of trance.

Maddox lowers his voice to ask, "And did you learn your lesson?" She clenches her thighs again and looks back at me before nodding to Maddox.

"But then you went and left him. That wasn't very nice, was it?"

Her gorgeous mouth parts and her tongue brushes along her bottom lip, her breathing shallow. Her chocolate eyes find mine and she shakes her head.

"What's that, kitten? Was that nice of you?"

"No Maddox, it wasn't nice at all." Her voice shifts

into a submissive tone, which makes my dick stand at attention. Our kitten wants to play. Maddox reaches out his hand and cups her chin. Her eyes find mine and I give her a reassuring smirk.

"Tell Blake you're sorry." His voice is low and even.

"I'm sorry, Blake. I shouldn't have left you."

"Good girl." He leans down and gives her a small, chaste kiss on the lips before stepping back. He's good at that.

I lean down and kiss her, nipping her bottom lip. She instantly parts for me, granting me entrance to her hot mouth. She pushes her small, curvy body against mine and haphazardly places the wine glass onto the counter so she can grip onto my shoulders.

I break away from our kiss and grab her hand to lead her with Maddox to the living room.

"Blake?" She sounds nervous. I bet she's never done anything like this before.

"Yeah, hellcat?" I sit next to Maddox on the sofa and pull her into my lap.

"I don't know what's going on." She looks up at me through her thick, dark lashes.

"Yeah you do. You want this?" I don't want to, but I have to give her an out. Once we get our hands on her, we're not letting go. She swallows thickly, looking at

Maddox then back at me. She nods her head slightly. "Say it. Tell me you want us to take you. You want us to fuck you." My dirty words make her breathing hitch. "Just know once we have you, we're not gonna let go." She clenches her thighs again and I can't resist the urge to slip my hand up her dress and brush my fingers along her heat. She moans at my touch.

"Yes. I want you." Her half-lidded eyes find Maddox's and she says, "I want both of you."

Maddox's voice drops as he gazes into Marie's chocolate brown eyes. "Come here, kitten. Blake owes you an orgasm."

MADDOX

It's a fucking dream come true, hearing my little kitten tell Blake that she wants both of us. I grab her hips and pull her off of Blake's lap and into mine.

"We're going to need to get rid of this." I don't hesitate to pull off her dress. I'm not going to hold back. She needs to know what she's getting herself into. She obediently lifts her arms to help me undress her.

I raise my brows at Blake while she tosses her clothes on the floor. Fuck yeah, she wants this. He grins as he lies on his back with his legs dangling over the armrest of the sofa. I see what he wants so I command our little kitten, "Put your pussy on Blake's tongue." She obeys, getting on all fours before sitting up. Her lips are already parted with her head thrown back. Blake's hands grab her thighs, with his fingers digging into her flesh. She angles her pussy so his lips are at her clit and rocks into him.

I turn on the sofa, sitting on my knees to grab her hips. "Ride him harder. I want you to cum on his tongue." I hear Blake lapping at her cunt and I find myself fucking jealous. I want my mouth on her gorgeous body so I lean forward and take her hardened, pink nipple into my mouth while kneading her other breast and plucking her nipple between my knuckles. She moans out her approval, panting heavily with both of her hands grabbing my shoulders for balance as I bite down on her left nipple and then the other. Her nails dig into my skin through my shirt and I fucking love it.

My other hand caresses, then helps steady her as she picks up her speed, steadily rocking on Blake's face. I can hear Blake feasting on her pussy like it's his last meal and I know she fucking loves it. I lean back, parting the seam of her lips with my tongue and sucking and massaging her tongue with mine. She moans her pleasure into my mouth as her body starts to tremble.

The sweet sound makes my rock-hard dick start leaking in my pants.

I stand up, leaving her to grip the sofa for balance, and start taking off my clothes while I watch her climax. Her one hand grips her breast, pulling her nipple and roughly massaging the plump flesh. Her head flies back as she screams out in ecstasy, stilling on Blake's tongue with her fingers digging into his scalp as her entire body trembles with desire.

It's the most gorgeous sight I've ever seen. I mentally store the sight of her cumming, hoping I never forget it.

As I stare, lips parted at my beautiful kitten, Blake slips out from under her and pushes her shoulders forward so she's on her knees with her head laying on the sofa, breathing heavily. His lips are swollen and glistening with her arousal. He doesn't even bother to wipe his mouth. Instead, he grabs her hips, forcing her ass in the air and he dives in, licking and sucking at her puckered hole. He pulls back to push a finger in and she pushes against him, moaning into the cushion.

"I can't fucking wait to cum in your ass." He slides a second finger in and starts finger fucking her ass. She's writhing on the sofa, but he steadies her with his hand on her hip.

I palm my dick and stroke it as I move toward her. I reach down with my other hand and pull her up by her shoulder. She rests on her elbows and her chocolate eyes find mine as she moans, parting those gorgeous lips.

"Wider." My voice is barely above a whisper, but it's still a command and she obeys immediately. I push my head in and pull back, just to give her a taste. Her tongue flicks out, licking the precum from my slit and I stifle my groan. Fuck! I grab her hair with my fist and push my length as far in as I can, feeling her throat stretch to fit my girth. Her tongue massages the underside of my dick as I slide in and out of her hot mouth. After only a few strokes, my spine starts to tingle and I have to pull out. I'm not ready to cum yet. No fucking way. I make my way under her body and kiss her as I get settled beneath her. I lick and suck on her lips before pushing my tongue in to explore that skilled mouth. She moans loud and sensual as I pull away.

"You're all ready for me, hellcat." She turns her head to look at Blake with her breath coming in shallow pants. He finds her eyes as he pushes the head of his cock into her tight hole. Her eyes widen and her mouth opens in a look of surprise and slight pain.

I reach between our bodies and my fingers find her

clit to rub while I tell her, "Push against him, kitten." She obeys, lowering her head to the crook of my neck while she stifles her moans.

Blake rocks in and out, giving her more of his dick each time. He's breathing hard too. I stroke my dick a few more times, watching the two of them exploring this new sensation together and reveling in it. He finally stills inside her ass once he's in her to the hilt.

"How's that feel?"

Marie doesn't lift her head when she responds, "So full. So good, but so full." Her hot breath tickles my neck.

"You're about to feel really full, kitten. Stay still." The head of my dick kisses the hot entrance to her sex and I move it to rub her clit with it, making her moan and suck on my neck. I dip back down between her wet pussy lips and push into her heat. "Fuck, you feel so fucking good." Her tight walls stretch as I enter her and she tries to wiggle away, but I still her by wrapping my other arm around her small frame. "Stay still." I lift my hips and slam into her, balls deep. Her neck arches and she screams in pleasure into the air above me. Without giving her time to adjust to my size or to having two cocks in her at the same time, I start pistoning into her, bucking my hips to crash against hers and gripping her thighs. Blake's holding onto her hips while he ruts into her ass.

Our kitten starts thrashing between us, lost in the intense mix of pleasure and pain. I find Marie's lips with mine to silence her screaming and continue rubbing her clit. Her teeth crash against mine in a brutal kiss. Blake reaches between us to play with her breasts and pull on her sensitive nipples. She breaks our kiss to moan out, "Too much." She starts shaking her head, breathing hard with her body trembling. I feel a cold sweat break out over my forehead and the tingling in my spine travels up my back as my balls draw up.

"Cum with us, Marie." She ignores my command, still violently shaking her head and moaning in ecstasy.

"Cum on Maddox's dick; let him feel how good you are." Blake's words send her over. A gush of warmth floods the space between our connection and her pussy clamps down on my dick, pulsing as her body spasms. I find my release with her, shooting waves of cum into her welcoming, throbbing heat. Blake slams his dick deeper in Marie's ass and stills, no doubt filling her ass, making her arch her back and whimper in pleasure with her eyes closed tight. I kiss and nip her neck and shoulder as the pulses of my orgasm subside, until she gently falls limp on my chest. Her shoulders rise and fall as she breathes deep, inhaling the scent of our passion.

After a moment of all of us reaching our peak in unison and catching our breaths, I feel Blake shift off of Marie and walk to the kitchen. I nuzzle into her fragile neck and kiss a small bruising mark one of us left on her. It makes me smile to know she's marked as ours. No one will have to wonder if our little kitten is owned. Blake comes back with a few wet paper towels in his hand. I slip out of her comforting heat and position Marie on the sofa belly down as he carefully wipes her down and massages her thighs and ass. I kiss her shoulder before finding my boxers.

Blake gives her ass a quick kiss before sliding his hands up her sides and leaving a trail of kisses to her shoulder. I hear him whisper in her ear, "You feeling alright, hellcat?" She hums a yes into the cushion before laying her cheek on the sofa, her deep brown eyes searching for ours. She finds Blake's eyes first and smiles before he leans down to give her a chaste kiss and then stands up. When her eyes find mine she gives me the same sweet smile and it makes my heart swell and beat against my chest with need. I kneel in front of her and rub my nose on hers, which makes her smile widen.

"Did you like that?" She nods her head, letting her forehead brush against mine.

"Yeah." She whispers the words between our lips and I kiss her gently.

"I'm glad you enjoyed it."

I hear Blake walk up beside me and say, "Now you're stuck with us."

Chapter 11

MARIE

"I'M SO FUCKING HAPPY YOU CAME WITH ME." I shift on the metal seat and bump my shoulder into Lexi. I instantly regret the rough movement. My pussy is so damn sore from the punishing fuck I took this morning.

"There's your crush." I raise my brows and stare at Jace so she can catch my gaze. As if on cue, he looks at us and gives Lexi a devilish grin. Lexi gives a small smile back and blushes before turning her attention to me.

"So you're *with* them?" she asks me ... *again*.

"I know it's weird, but," I gesture aimlessly and falter over what to say next.

"I mean I get it," Lexi says quickly and puts up her

hands as if to say she's not judging. "They're obviously… into you."

"And they get me," I say pointedly. It's been two weeks since Blake and Maddox claimed me as theirs and I've never been happier. "It wasn't supposed to turn into this. I can't even believe it's more than like…" I huff out a breath and blow at the stray lock of hair dangling in my face.

"Than a quick, dirty fuck?" she asks in a hushed tone with her eyes all over Jace. He keeps taking peeks at her too and it makes me smile that much wider.

"I mean it though; I didn't expect this."

She's slow to turn and look at me as the seconds pass, but when she does she offers me an easy smile. "Some happily ever afters come super fast and are smutty as hell." She looks back at the boys and adds, "Good for you."

I can't help but to smile. Maybe it's too soon to say it's love.

But it's more than lust. And I know I want more. I want so much more.

MADDOX

"We can't just knock her up."

"I didn't say that," I say defensively. Blake keeps

looking at me like I'm the one who's crazy. And as he shuts the door to the office and flicks on the light, part of me wonders if maybe I am.

"You implied it," he spits back and rummages through the drawer to his desk. My brow furrows; I don't know what we're looking for or why we're even here.

"I'm just saying …" I trail off as I try to word it right. I want to keep our kitten. She needs to stay. And the only thing I can think of is to put a baby in her.

"We have an unconventional relationship. In a lot of ways. But fuck anyone who has the time to give a shit." He says the words like it's just natural not to care. To take it easy and slow and that's where he'll fuck up.

He'll let her get away because he'll be too happy to see it coming.

"She's going to want something different." I talk to his back as he finally stops digging in the drawer.

"No, she's going to want something more. Not different," he says and then turns to me holding out his hand.

"What's that?" I ask him without moving. I'm leaning with my back against the wall as I stare at his closed fist.

"Take it," he says then shakes his hand and I shake my head in return.

All I can imagine is that it's something from back when he was in the PD. He's retired now, officially. And as far as anyone else knows, he's no one special but a man with tattoos, who likes to ride a Harley.

And with a lot of friends who like the same.

"What is it?" I ask him again and he gives me an exasperated look.

"It was my mom's," he answers and then opens his hand, palm up to reveal a simple ring. "I don't think it's really her taste, but we can add to it," he says while I take in the round stone and rose gold band.

"I think she'd love it," I tell him in an even voice even though I can feel my heart squeezing in my chest. One ring. And this one has meaning.

"You'll have to get her the band the same day," he says and his words force my gaze back to his.

"A band?"

"You know, the other ring."

"That's for the wedding day," I tell him and clench my jaw even though I'm all emotional for no good reason.

"I say we do it all at once."

"You serious?" I ask him even though I already know the answer. There's no way we're letting her go.

"That's how she likes it," Blake says as if it's the obvious answer, and I have to laugh at his words.

"Shit, that's how all three of us like it," I say, finally feeling a little easier.

"First the rings, then the babies." He shuts the door and slips the ring into his pocket.

I nod my head, thinking about Marie's belly and everything that's to come. "Alright then. Rings first, and then the babies."

Thank you for reading this smutty, dirty novella. I usually don't write quickies, but I have to admit this was fun and put a smile on my face. If you love fast-paced romantic suspense with a dark edge and angst to boot, you'll love any one of my novels.

Happy reading and best wishes,
Willow xx

About Willow Winters

Thank you so much for reading my romances. I'm just a stay at home mom and avid reader turned author and I couldn't be happier.

I hope you love my books as much as I do!

More by Willow Winters
WWW.WILLOWWINTERSWRITES.COM/BOOKS

www.ingramcontent.com/pod-product-compliance
Lightning Source LLC
LaVergne TN
LVHW090811291125
826635LV00007B/14